LAST THINGS

LAST THINGS

Paul McCusker

Augustine Institute
Greenwood Village, CO

Augustine Institute
6160 S. Syracuse Way, Suite 310
Greenwood Village, CO 80111
Tel: (866) 767-3155
www.augustineinstitute.org

Cover Design: Zander Renault

Last Things is an extensive revision of the previously
published *Pap's Place*, *The Faded Flower*, and
The Faded Flower Christmas Show.

28 27 26 25 24 23 22   2 3 4 5 6 7

ISBN: 978-1-955305-20-4
Library of Congress Control Number: 2021945702

Printed in Canada ⊗

For Chester Freed, Minnie Lyons, and Jack Davis,
in whose memories this book is lovingly dedicated.

CONTENTS

Prologue
That Day

THAT DAY, the one when everything changed for the Reynolds family, started out as normal as normal could be. Michael Reynolds had showered and dressed for work, his mind pressing ahead to the day's first meeting at the office. Something to do with employee benefits.

His wife, Colleen, dressed in the thick pink robe the kids had given her for Christmas several years before, was softly humming while moving between the coffee maker and the toaster.

His son, Ethan, fumbled around with a backpack, half-heartedly checking to make sure the right books were there for the day's college classes.

His daughter, Madison, was on her phone, thumbing through the various messages and posts from the many social apps that demanded her attention. Her backpack was all ready to go for another day in tenth grade.

There was no hint, no omen, no foreshadowing of what was to come. The day ran like every other weekday. The little moments ticked along with a reassuring banality.

At three o'clock, when Colleen retrieved the day's mail, she had no idea that the beige envelope from Michael's aunt Minnie contained important news.

At four o'clock, Michael didn't know about Aunt Minnie's letter, nor could he know what was about to happen when he walked into his boss's office.

By five o'clock, that day would be forever marked as *that day*.

PART ONE

POP'S PLACE

CHAPTER 1

MICHAEL STOOD in his boss's office and thought, as he often had, that it looked like the set of a nightly talk show. There was the obligatory mahogany desk and fake plants and mural covering the wall with some beauty spot in Hawaii. Michael's boss, a man sadly named Harold Mole, had taken the picture while on vacation, and then had it reproduced onto the wall through the wonders of modern graphic technology. Unfortunately, the modern graphic technology did not remove the shadow of Harold's thumb from the far right edge. Harold had left it, declaring that it was his "signature."

"Like Alfred Hitchcock appearing in his own movies," Harold had said.

Most people thought of it as a silly mistake.

Michael thought about other mistakes as he looked at his boss's name plate on the desk. *Harold Mole.* What were Mr. and Mrs. Mole thinking? Harold Mole easily became *Harry Mole*. What must life had been like for the poor boy in school?

Worse, the name suited him. He was short, with bushy gray hair over his ears and under his nose, and a frumpy look that stayed with him no matter what he wore. He was friendly enough, in the way dull, non-offensive people are. When he got emphatic, as he sometimes did when talking about sports or politics or in motivational meetings, he jabbed his forefinger in the air and used "people" a lot. "All right, *people*, we need to think outside of the box, get in the right zone, and maximize our potential. Or, *as I like to say*, let's give one-hundred-and-ten percent!"

In spite of the name, Michael liked Harold Mole. *Amiable* was the word Michael might use to describe their relationship. Until now.

Now, Harold paced behind his desk without making eye contact. He had begun a run-on sentence about the impact on them all because of the acquisition of the company just last year by a New York conglomerate.

Michael waited for the bad news. Maybe the New York company was increasing the pressure for better sales numbers, or more profitable book signings. Or maybe it was a problem with one of their departments. Michael thought about his own editorial team, but couldn't imagine any issues there.

Michael's eye wandered to the window and the line of Rocky Mountains in the distance. A cold front had cleared away Denver's smog and left the snow-covered ridges in sharp relief against the blue sky. Then he focused closer, on the sign to the company in front of the building with the logo for the Bradlow Publishing Company. The logo was a *B* that rested on an open book. It had been designed in the 1950s—and looked like it. Maybe it was cutting edge then, but it now looked outdated.

Give it time, Harold once said. *In another ten years, that very same logo will look trendy again. It'll be considered retro-classic.*

Michael doubted it. It looked like it had been designed by a fifteen-year-old artist—and had. David Bradlow's oldest daughter, in 1957. *She's in her seventies now*, Michael thought.

They'd had the chance to change the logo when the company moved into its current headquarters in the early '90s. Mr. Bradlow himself was adamant about keeping it as it was. A lost opportunity.

Looking up, Michael suddenly realized that Harold had stopped to take a breath. Had he asked Michael a question? Had Michael missed something while thinking about the company logo?

Apparently not. Harold continued with "And so ..." and the news was dropped into the middle of his next run-on sentence like a small pebble in a large river.

"I'm sorry. What did you say?" Michael had to ask.

Harold loudly cleared his throat and explained that *New York*— not the city itself, of course, but the conglomerate—now wanted to consolidate various services at their headquarters there. "Editorial Acquisitions will be based there, with only two people maintaining the department here. You're not one of the two, Michael."

"What?" Michael said, trying to comprehend what he'd just heard. "You're letting me go?"

"It's nothing personal," Harold said. "You're good, but they want someone who has that New York snap-crackle-and-pop. Not west-of-the-Mississippi corn flakes. I'm really sorry. It's just a practical business decision."

"Move me to another department, then," Michael said.

"I can't. We have all the people they'll let us keep."

Michael stared at Harold.

"You would have made the same decision yourself if you were in their shoes," Harold added. "Anyway, the severance package is generous and there is always the windfall from the profit-sharing. Stocks went up with the buy-out. Michelle will explain it all to you."

Harold continued to talk, his voice becoming a drone in the background as Michael sank further into the burgundy faux leather guest chair. He felt queasy. A numbness seemed to be taking over his brain.

"*Michelle?*" he said, a delayed reaction.

"Michelle from HR. She flew in from New York. It was inevitable, Michael. I'm surprised you didn't see it coming."

True, Michael thought, *I should have seen it coming*. And a wave of self-recrimination washed over him.

Harold leaned forward and spoke in a low, conspiratorial tone. "Look, I don't expect anything to be left of the Bradlow Publishing Company within five years. New York will absorb everything. Consider yourself lucky to get out now."

Lucky? Michael might have felt lucky if he'd been given the five years to prepare.

The numb feeling in his brain now niggled at his chest. He'd been with Bradlow Books since college. No, before that, if you counted his summer internship there. He'd spent over thirty years rising through the ranks. And he'd expected to be there until his retirement. He was loyal to the company. A lifer. He never cared for all the moving around that other professionals did. He had deflected other job opportunities to stay with them. Denver was his home. Didn't that mean anything anymore?

"How can they do this to me?" Michael asked, the words clicking loudly from his dry mouth.

"I'm sorry," Harold said. He looked relieved, as if he felt better now that the bad news was off his shoulders and on someone else's.

He looked at his watch and made a face as if to say *Please don't make a scene; I have a dinner engagement right after work.*

Michael stood up. His legs and feet felt like rubber bands attached to cement blocks. Michelle, the director of human resources, stood in the doorway. "Let's go down to my office," she said.

Michael walked behind her with his head down, not out of embarrassment, but to make sure he didn't stumble. Mercifully, the halls and stairwell were clear. It was now after five o'clock. Had everyone gone home, or were they hiding from the dead man walking?

I should have known, Michael thought, berating himself again. When the conglomerate made the offer to buy Bradlow, and Mr. Bradlow himself explained how good it would be for the shareholders and employees, Michael should have seen the handwriting on the wall.

Except the handwriting was never actually on a wall. It had been buried in the friendly and cordial corporate emails that came promising minimal impact to the personnel, the value of such great talent to the combined strengths of the two companies, and how much they looked forward to working with each and every one of them into a long and profitable future. Michael had believed it all.

Forms for his termination, forms for his benefits, forms for his severance, forms for unemployment, forms to acknowledge that he had handed over his keys, forms to promise that he would not take any company property or data with him, forms to assess the termination process, forms to acknowledge receipt of the forms.... He nodded and signed with Michelle's sympathetic expression hanging like a shadow over it all.

"Go home. Take time to process this change," she said, making it sound like a generous offer even though it was time to go home anyway.

Michael walked across the department to his office. His secretary was gone. No doubt Michelle had warned her, allowing a chance to escape any awkward scenes. He wondered if she would be terminated, too. He hadn't thought to ask. How selfish.

He heard a noise in his office and looked through the doorway to see two of the maintenance staff putting his personal things into a banker's box. They saw him, looked petrified that they'd been caught doing it, and, with mumbles of condolences, hurried out.

He closed the office door and paused to take a deep breath. A clock on a now-empty shelf ticked loudly. Take a moment to think, he decided. Sitting down in his chair, he clasped his hands on the armrests and pivoted back and forth, back and forth. He closed his eyes. He opened them again. The office with its wooden bookcases and credenza, the in-box and computer monitor, came in and out of view.

How will I tell Colleen?

Just then, there was knock at his door. Michael stood up. Clarence, the elderly security guard, pushed the door open.

"Just checking," Clarence said.

The two men nodded to each other. It was nothing personal, Michael knew. Just a precaution to make sure that a disgruntled employee wasn't sabotaging anything on the way out.

Michael ran his hands over his forehead and through his thick brown-and-gray hair. He yanked at his tie and undid the top button of his white oxford shirt.

He gestured to the banker's box. "They do good work," he said to Clarence, referring to the two maintenance men. He pulled opened the various drawers and checked the shelves. "I think they got it all."

I wish they had let me do it, he thought. Packing would have helped him contain the disaster somehow; bring order to the disorder. And, for a moment, he remembered the morning of his mother's funeral and how he was irrationally filled with the desire—the *need*—to reorganize the collection of knickknacks on her bookshelf. He arranged them according to size. Everyone thought he was crazy—except his father. His father simply put a hand on his shoulder and said, "Thank you. Your mother had been meaning to do that for a long time."

Michael stared at the banker's box and thought, *Three decades reduced to a single box*. It was like his career had been cremated.

Clarence stepped into the office. "Well," he said, meaning "time to go." His eyes reflected a genuine sadness.

"Right," said Michael.

"Mr. Reynolds." Clarence's voice was a low growl. "I can't tell you ..." And he didn't.

Michael nodded. "If I missed anything, I'm sure they'll send it to my house."

"I'm sure they will." Clarence shuffled uncomfortably.

A smile crept onto Michael's face. He wondered what Clarence would do if he actually went rock star–crazy and began to trash the office. The poor man would probably have a heart attack.

Clarence's face flushed as he said, "It's not right, you know, sneaking you out at the end of the day like this."

Michael opened his mouth to explain all the reasons companies did it this way. With a jolt, he realized he didn't have to defend the company's practices. It wasn't his company anymore.

"Thank you," he managed to say.

Clarence nervously jingled the keys in his pocket.

Michael grabbed his coat and his briefcase. He turned to take the box, but Clarence had already picked it up. *Kind man.* They saw no one during the journey from the office to the elevator and down to the front lobby. He knew people were still working in the building.

Clarence, clutching the box by both handles, pushed open the front door with his hip and allowed Michael to go through. It was early November and already dark. The sun was hidden behind the Rocky Mountains now. The air was crisp, even bracing.

Once the box was in the back seat of Michael's car, Clarence held out his hand. "God bless," he said. "I'll be praying for you."

In all the time he'd known Clarence, Michael had never said a word about religion, though he attended Mass regularly. He knew Clarence was a churchgoer—an Evangelical Protestant—because he often saw an open Bible on Clarence's desk. He believed Clarence really would pray for him.

Michael shook the old man's hand gratefully. Even Harold Mole hadn't offered him a handshake.

In his car, Michael sat behind the steering wheel and watched Clarence walk back to the red brick building. The doors closed and Clarence became a blurred image behind the glass, his movements suggesting he was locking the doors.

Michael remembered when he had first walked through the front doors of that small outpost in the world of publishing. The doors were ornately carved oak back then. Now they were glass. The offices were cozy then, but were eventually replaced by cubicles. Since that first day, he had married Colleen and fathered two children, now young adults themselves.

In a second-story window, he saw the silhouette of Harold Mole looking out of his executive window. He didn't have a pressing dinner engagement after all.

Michael started his car and pulled away. He kept his eyes focused straight ahead, ignoring the burning that threatened to become tears.

The Bradlow Company was nestled in an office complex in Littleton, the suburb of Denver where Michael lived. Normally, he made it home in less than twenty minutes. Today, he was stopped at every red light and had to detour around a fender-bender blocking the main road into his neighborhood. The twenty minutes stretched to thirty. It gave him time to think, to be rational, to plan.

Instead, a voice screamed in his head, *It's not fair, it's not fair, it's not fair!* as he sat at an intersection and pounded his steering wheel.

A woman in a minivan one lane over looked at him with alarm. In the back, two children were pointing at him and laughing.

He tried to turn the pounding into something rhythmic, as if he was rocking out to a song on the radio.

The kids laughed even more.

The woman shook her head at him as she pulled away from the light.

He wrapped his hands around the steering wheel until his knuckles were white. He reminded himself that fairness had little to do with real life. To think otherwise was childish.

It doesn't make sense, it doesn't make sense, it doesn't make sense became the new mantra.

Well, yes, of course it made sense. Small publishing companies were nearly extinct. The conglomerates swallowed up everything that looked successful. Digital publishing by individuals took the rest. Michael should have seen it coming.

But their "good business sense" had now changed his life. How would he find another job at his age?

I don't even know how to write a résumé, he thought. *Do people even look at résumés anymore? They must. Digitally. Somewhere.*

He felt like a man who now had to face dating after years of marriage. What were the rules? What was expected of him?

Michael thought about God. All his life, he'd made it a point not to take the good things for granted. *Give thanks to God for he is good*, a Bible verse said. Be grateful to God. And Michael was grateful. God had given him a loving wife, reasonably manageable kids, a decent living, and a secure job. God was on his throne, and the universe—at least Michael's—was well-ordered and sensible. In response, Michael did what he could for God. He attended church—in fact, he had served on each of the church committees over the years, including a brief stint as the treasurer. He ushered, tithed, gave to the poor, read the daily Bible reading, and prayed an Our Father every morning. So, what went wrong?

I thought we had an understanding, Michael complained to God. *What are you thinking?*

By the time Michael pulled into his garage, God had not replied.

He stopped the engine and rehearsed how to break the news to Colleen. "Hi, honey. Guess who gets to write his résumé tonight?" or "You're not going to believe what happened today!" or "Sit down, darling. I have some bad news."

Should he tell her nonchalantly, as if it didn't really matter? Or should he sit her down, phrase the words carefully, and assure her by his positive expressions and light tone of voice that all would be well?

He thought of the times his friends had been fired and the manicured phrases he'd used in the name of comfort.

Michael left everything in the car as he carefully opened the door into the house. He could smell the pasta Colleen was making for dinner. He imagined her reaction. She would be sympathetic. She would be reassuring and supportive. She would be strong. But he knew deep inside she'd be emotionally wringing her hands and wondering what to do. He hated for her to worry. It would be so much better if he could fix the situation: find another job, then tell her after it was done.

Sighing, he stepped through the laundry room and into the kitchen. As always, the countertops were spotless, as if the house were on permanent display to sell. *That may be useful,* he thought— then cringed.

* * *

Colleen was sitting at the small breakfast table just beyond the kitchen. Her hands were folded serenely in front of her. Her glasses and a piece of notepaper were trapped underneath them. A Bible sat off to the side. She was in profile as she gazed out the small panels of windows in the French doors leading into the back yard. Her light brown hair was tied up, and she wore an oversized denim shirt. Even at this moment Michael marveled over how little she'd changed since he'd met her in college. The laugh lines around her blue eyes were deeper, but she hadn't lost the freshness of her face. Considering what she'd been through with her alcoholic parents— both eventually dying from the physical effects of their addictions— her bright looks and positive attitude were nothing short of a miracle. Michael wished he had a picture of her right then.

Poker face, he thought. *I need my best poker face.*

He stepped closer. She turned, smiling, and then took one look at him and her smile vanished.

That's why I always lose at poker.

"Hi," he said, as if he had to honor the *husband and wife greeting ritual* before he could entertain questions. He tossed his coat over a chair. She tilted her face up and he kissed her.

"Hi," she said. "Something has happened."

Michael eyed her a moment and wondered if someone from the office had called her with the news, maybe the wife of a co-worker.

"Why do you say that?" He was being coy, but his curiosity was piqued about what she knew and how she knew it.

Colleen picked up the notepaper. "We got a letter from Aunt Minnie today."

He was puzzled. *Aunt Minnie couldn't know about my job.* He asked, "How is Aunt Minnie?"

"She wants to give your father a party for his eightieth birthday."

Birthday parties—at a time like this? Michael couldn't think about that now. "We'll see," he said.

Colleen looked up at him. "She *really* needs us to come."

"*Needs?* I get the importance of an eightieth birthday, but..." He let the sentence trail off for Colleen to finish for herself. Then he opened the refrigerator to find something to drink. His mouth had gone dry.

"She needs us to come for another reason," Colleen said, her tone serious.

Michael grabbed a can of soda. He didn't want to talk about Aunt Minnie's letter. But his wife's tone made him look around the refrigerator door at her. His expression presented the unspoken question.

"Aunt Minnie says your father has Alzheimer's disease," Colleen said.

Michael closed the refrigerator door and did a double take—an honest-to-goodness, straight-from-the-movies double take. He could almost hear the *wagga-wagga* sound effect like they put in the cartoons. "He ... *what*?"

She held up the letter. "He's been showing the symptoms over the past few months. Dr. Janssen did some cognitive tests and wants to do an MRI."

Michael took the letter and glanced at his aunt's neat Peterson-method cursive writing. He was dumbfounded. "She actually persuaded him to submit to tests?"

Colleen nodded. "Dr. Janssen is worried he'll hurt himself if he's not put into some kind of care," she said. "He can't live alone anymore. It's not safe. Aunt Minnie wants us to come and talk to him."

It was too much for Michael to think about. "Talk to him? About what? What can we say to him?"

"He needs to move into a retirement home, or assisted living, or whatever they're called these days." Colleen's face looked pinched now, her eyes watering.

"Move out of his house?" Michael shook his head. Not his father. Not in a million years. Michael plucked at the tab on the can of soda. It spat briefly and then exploded in a wild spray. He shouted, holding the can away from him like a live hand grenade. He spun to the sink and dropped the can with a hiss, fizz, and clatter.

Colleen grabbed at the paper towels and quickly dampened a handful. She knelt to wipe the floor. Michael picked up a hand towel to dab at his white shirt. *Will I ever wear white shirts again?* he wondered.

With his back to her, he said, "I guess this makes the perfect end to a perfect day."

"I'll take your suit to the dry cleaners tomorrow." She scrubbed at the floor. *Swish, swish, swish.*

"I won't need this suit tomorrow. Or even the day after that. Or maybe ever," Michael said.

"Why not?"

"I've been let go."

Swish, swish—silence.

Michael looked over at his wife. She was frozen in the middle of the kitchen floor, her head down, clutching the soda-saturated paper towel.

"Did you hear me?" he asked.

Her reaction was completely unexpected. At first, she made a sound that might have been a sigh that turned into a groan. She sat back on her legs. She put her free hand to her mouth. Then she turned to him with a look of wonder on her face.

Michael leaned against the counter and folded his arms. He was mystified. "Did I miss something?"

"I had lunch with Sally," Colleen said.

Spooky Sally from church, Michael thought. The woman often claimed to have visions and messages that she called "words from the Lord." She gave Michael the creeps.

Colleen continued, "She said she had been praying for us the other day. She suddenly got a 'picture' of us moving away from here and living in your father's house. At the time, I thought she had gotten her wires crossed. Then I got Aunt Minnie's letter and ..."

"I wouldn't put a lot of stock in what she says."

Colleen lowered her head, poised to finish mopping up his mess. Then her shoulders started to heave and the sobs began. Michael sat down on the floor next to her and pulled her close.

"But I hate hospitals," she said, crying into his neck.

Michael remembered vividly what she'd gone through with her father. "I know," he said, and closed his eyes. He breathed in deeply and could smell a hint of lavender in her hair.

"And I hate unemployment offices," he said.

———◆———

It was getting harder and harder for the Reynolds family to sit down together for a meal, but Colleen texted Ethan and Madison and made it clear they were having dinner *at home* so they could talk about some *very important things.* The kids were inclined to push back with Michael or ignore his texts altogether. Never Colleen's.

Michael studied his two children as they sat down to eat their lasagna. Ethan favored Colleen's side of the family with their fair features, large eyes, upturned noses, and light brown wavy hair. He was a heartbreakingly handsome boy except for the wispy goatee, which, in Michael's opinion, made him look like an alley cat. Ethan didn't seem to care. Why worry about his looks when he spent all his time on a computer? Interaction with flesh-and-blood people, social skills, hygiene ... what did they matter to Ethan?

Madison, on the other hand, got her looks from Michael's side of the family. There were times when she resembled Michael's mother at a lost age. She'd flick at her dark brown hair or tilt her head in such a way that transported Michael back in time to his childhood, when his mother still had her youthful features. Madison also had his mother's dark eyes and a button nose that made her face look wider than it was. A distinctive dimple to the right of her mouth gave the impression that she was always on the verge of a smile. Like most girls her age, she had mood swings but most of the time she was even-keeled, good-natured, and friendly.

Both of his kids were. Most of the time.

After they said grace and took only a few bites of their food, Michael announced that he'd been let go.

The news was met with an awkward silence, side-glances, and random stabs at the pasta.

Then Ethan shook his head and said, "Typical. Big business. Nothing personal, no humanity. Wall Street wins."

"Are we going to have to move?" Madison asked.

Michael leaned back in his chair. "That depends. If I find a job in the area, then no. If I don't—"

"I *want* to move," Madison said. "I'm really sick and tired of living here."

"You're sick and tired of *Meghan*," Ethan corrected her.

"Meghan? But she's your best friend," Colleen said to Madison. "If we moved, you'd miss her."

"No, I wouldn't," Madison said.

Ethan snorted loudly and rolled his eyes.

Madison threw a dinner roll at him. "She's so annoying! She won't stop teasing me."

"Teasing you about what?" asked Colleen.

"Because I'm not allowed to get a tattoo," she said, then slowly turned her gaze to her father.

Michael eyed his daughter wearily. "You're going to bring that up at a time like this?"

Madison shrugged as a wry smile crossed her face. "It was worth a try."

"I think losing your job is the best thing that could happen to you," Ethan said. "Now you can do what you *really* want to do."

"I was doing what I really wanted to do," Michael said.

"You didn't like your job," Ethan said.

"Yes, I did."

"No, you didn't. I heard you say so to Mom. They took you from finding worthwhile books to finding authors of books about high school testing and HR policies. I mean, how could you *like* sitting behind a desk day after day?"

Michael stared at his son with disbelief. "And who is it that sits at his computer for hours on end looking at videos of people doing stupid things?"

"We're not talking about me right now; we're talking about you," Ethan said, undaunted. "Just look at the garage, Dad. All those tools and that machinery you bought for your workbench. Isn't that what you really like to do? Fix things? *Make* things? Isn't that what you do every weekend?"

"It's a hobby, Ethan," Michael explained in a measured tone. "There's a difference between a job and a hobby."

Ethan shoved a forkful of salad into his mouth. "Why?"

Michael shook his head. "I don't want to talk about this now." He said to Colleen, "Give them the rest of the news."

Colleen told the kids about the letter from Aunt Minnie.

Ethan looked surprised. "A *handwritten* letter? Delivered in the *mailbox*?"

"With a stamp and everything," Colleen teased.

"A birthday party would be fun," Madison said.

Michael looked aghast at his two children. "Didn't you hear what your mom said? Pop might have Alzheimer's disease."

"Do you know what that is?" Colleen asked them.

"Of course I do," Madison said and turned to her brother. "Tell them, Ethan."

Ethan looked down at his lap as if in deep concentration. "It's a disease. A progressive brain disorder. Irreversible."

"You're cheating!" Madison said. She pointed to Ethan's hands. "He's looking at his phone. Well, I can do that, too." And like a magician pulling cards out of thin air, she produced a phone in her hands and began thumbing at the screen.

"No devices at the table!" Colleen protested.

"It's the only way to have an informed discussion," Ethan said.

Madison read from her phone: "Alzheimer's leads to dementia, which is the loss of cognitive functions, like ordered thinking and remembering and reasoning." She smiled at Ethan. "I guess you've had it most of your life."

"Ho, ho," Ethan said.

Colleen folded her napkin and placed it next to her plate. "So, what's our plan?"

"Plan?" Ethan asked. "What kind of plan do we need? We're going to Pop's party."

"And Dad has to find a job," Madison added.

"Or maybe Dad won't get a job and we'll have to move in with Pop, just like Spooky Sally said." Ethan smiled at his father.

Michael shot Colleen a disapproving look. He really wished she hadn't told them about that.

"I like Hope Springs," Madison said, referring to the small town where Pop had lived all his life—and her father's home for the first eighteen years of his. "I'd like to live there."

"There aren't any colleges near Hope Springs," Colleen said.

Ethan shrugged. "College is overrated. She'll do all right without it."

Michael turned to his son. "I suppose one of your *hobbies* will pay the bills?"

"Sure. Why not? Henry Ford. Bill Gates. Steve Jobs. They didn't finish college."

"You're going to be one of those?" Michael asked.

Ethan grinned. "It could happen."

"In which area will you excel, in particular?" Michael asked. "High scores on a computer game? Time spent on social apps? Watching mindless videos?"

"Somebody is making money from them," said Ethan.

"Maybe a few people," Michael countered. "But the chances of being one of the few that finds success is like winning the lottery. You need a real job, with a college degree as your backup. You won't get anywhere in business without it."

"Like you did?" Ethan asked.

There was a collective intake of breath between Colleen and Madison.

Stung, Michael simply stared at his son.

Ethan pushed his fork around his plate for a moment. "I said that wrong. I didn't mean ... uh ..." His sentence turned into a mumble and faded away.

Michael got up from the table and took his dishes to the kitchen. Standing silently at the sink, he fumed because his son wasn't completely wrong. He had dedicated himself to a company and look where it landed him.

What am I going to do?

Chapter 2

In the time leading up to the trip to Hope Springs for Pop's party, Michael used the internet to remind himself how to write a new résumé. He did the necessary work, with appropriate embellishments to his phrasing, then sent the document out to every contact he had in the publishing world. Then he reworked the résumé to explore options beyond publishing, hoping his skills with interpersonal relationships could serve him elsewhere.

He waited a couple of days before phoning his contacts directly. The conversations followed a consistent pattern: great to hear from you, sorry to hear the news, bad timing what with a lot of belt-tightening in the industry, no positions available, hope it all works out.

It was Brad Mayers, an old friend from another publishing house, who put it in perspective. "It's your age, Michael."

"I'm only fifty-four!"

Michael could hear Brad sip his coffee. "That puts you thirty years older than people they can hire fresh from college—and pay a lot less."

"Doesn't experience count for anything?"

"Not as much as we experienced people like to think."

"Then what am I supposed to do?"

"Try one of the coastal companies: New York, Boston, Washington, San Francisco, Los Angeles."

"Too far. My family wants to stay in Colorado."

"Try consulting, then. Find your angle and sell that to the smaller companies. Then you can work your way up to the big ones."

Soon after that conversation, Michael began to wake up in the middle of the night short of breath. It was as if the room had simply run out of air. And once he was awake, his mind went through all of the worst possible options for his future: ransack his retirement accounts, sell the house, take a job at a fast-food restaurant working next to his kids' friends.

He thought of Spooky Sally. What if she was right? What if he'd wind up back where he started—Hope Springs?

Some nights he made the mistake of looking online at websites, posts, and bulletin boards. Unemployed men wrote about the loss of hope, their mental health issues, depression, anger, failed marriages, substance abuse, even desire for suicide. A decade of his Rosary was the only shield to keep from falling into those feelings.

Other nights he went to the garage and started to build a bookcase. Maybe building something was the one thing in his life where he felt he had control. The wood was cooperative, if he respected it. The saws, the bits, the lathes, all performed as expected. Measurements were not argumentative. Everything did what he needed it to do, according to plan.

Colleen, meanwhile, coordinated the birthday party via telephone with Aunt Minnie. Minnie was Pop's sister-in-law. At eighty-two, she was the oldest member of the entire family, but she had all the vibrancy of a woman half her age. Her only issue was talking on the phone. She struggled to operate her "new" flip-phone, preferred to use her landline, but often got confused by her answering machine, which picked up after only two rings and recorded her and the caller saying "Hello?" and "Wait a minute" while Minnie's own recorded voice told them both to leave a message. At times, she was never quite sure which contraption was ringing to get her attention. Michael made a mental note to change the settings on her answering machine when he got into town.

Aunt Minnie was "thrilled beyond repair" that they were coming, she had said. Colleen noticed, though, that she always seemed to avoid any discussion about Pop's condition. "That'll keep until you get here," she would say.

"What about Dennis?" Colleen asked Michael one evening. Dennis was Michael's older brother, now living in Houston. "Aunt Minnie thinks it'd be wonderful if he could make a surprise appearance."

"Fat chance," Michael said. Dennis had left Hope Springs at the age of sixteen for a stint in the Army. Afterward, he took a job with an oil company, and then another, and rose through the ranks by leaping from one corporate ladder to another. Michael was never sure who Dennis worked for, or where he might be found at any given moment. He might be in Europe. Maybe the Middle East. Maybe South America.

"You should call him so he knows what's going on," Colleen said.

Michael begrudgingly agreed, though he knew the outcome before the call connected. His brother was pleasant, cordial, sympathetic, but didn't think he could come back unless it was an emergency.

"In other words, don't call you unless he dies," Michael said.

The line hissed for a moment. "You don't have to put it like that."

"We were hard-pressed to get you back for Mom's funeral."

"That wasn't my fault. I was closing a deal in Bahrain."

"Where are you now?" Michael asked.

More hissing line. "Look, there's nothing I can do right now. Have fun at the birthday party. Let me know how it goes. Call me if things get really bad."

"Oh, and I forgot to tell you that I was let go the other day," Michael said. It was hard to admit. Dennis would surely view it as a personal failure on Michael's part.

The hissing on the call went to a dead silence.

Michael looked at the screen. The call had disconnected.

While he was looking at his phone, it rang again. It wasn't Dennis. It was Pop.

"Hi, Dad," Michael said.

"So, when are you coming up to see me?" he asked. These were always his first words.

"Oh, I don't know. Sometime soon, maybe."

"My birthday's just around the corner, you know."

"Really? I'll remind Colleen to send a card."

"Send yourselves," he said. "I think Minnie is trying to cook something up. A surprise. She needs to be careful surprising me at this age. Ben—you remember Ben—walked into his house, they all yelled 'Surprise!' and he dropped dead of a heart attack. Died on the spot. But it was a still a great party. They used the leftover cake at his funeral."

"We'll see what we can do."

"How's work?"

Had Aunt Minnie mentioned to Pop about his job? "Things are a little quiet right now," Michael replied.

"Good. Then there's no reason not to visit."

"How are *you* doing?" Michael asked.

"My knee's been stiff lately. I think there's a storm front coming. A lot of snow, they say. Halloween won't be much fun for the kids."

"Halloween was a couple of weeks ago."

"Was it?" Pop paused. "I don't know where the time goes. You know my birthday is coming up."

"Yes, Dad, you just said so."

"I did?" he asked. "To who?"

"To me."

"When?"

"Just now."

"Well, it doesn't hurt to keep reminding you. Then maybe you'll come to visit."

"Maybe."

Michael wondered if his father's forgetfulness was a symptom of Alzheimer's or his age. How long had he been repeating himself in conversations? How many times had he told the same story of something that had happened in town? How often had he mentioned that so-and-so had died, or his struggles with the weeds in the yard, or the rabbits that kept attacking his flower bed?

"Are you still there, Michael?" Pop asked.

"I'm here."

"Did you hear the one about the drunk who was about to go into a bar? A street preacher stopped him and said, 'Stop, friend! The devil is in there!' The drunk slurred, 'Well, if he is, he's buying his own drinks!'"

Michael laughed politely, though he'd heard that joke from his father more times than he could count. This was how his Dad said goodbye.

"I'll talk to you soon, Dad."

"Goodbye, son."

Michael hung up. Maybe he should call Dr. Janssen to get a better perspective about his father's actual condition—and how to deal with the problem.

The next day he learned that Colleen was already a step ahead of him. She had been scouring the many websites and had ordered a few books about the disease.

"Alois Alzheimer, a German physician, discovered it early in the twentieth century," she told him. "Before then, people were called senile, scatter-brained, or 'doddering.' Sometimes they were declared insane. One in ten Americans over the age of sixty-five suffers from it. Two-thirds of them are women. After heart disease, cancer, and strokes, Alzheimer's comes next."

She went on to explain that its attack on the brain not only reduced memory and cognitive thinking but also affected language, diminished motor skills, and even changed a person's personality. Paranoia was common among patients, irrational anger with physical violence sometimes followed. Maybe it was genetic, maybe not. Maybe it had to do with proteins, maybe not. What the experts didn't know was greater than what they did. "There are ways to fight the symptoms, but no cure," she concluded.

Michael listened attentively. He tried to line up those facts with the father he'd known all his life. He braced himself for what he'd encounter in Hope Springs.

Gasping for air, Michael sat up in bed. He blinked at the darkness.

Colleen moved next to him. She took his hand in hers.

When he got his breath back, he said, "Maybe we shouldn't talk about Alzheimer's before I go to sleep."

"We're facing a lot of stress," she said softly. "We should pray together more."

He gave a noncommittal grunt.

"You don't want to?"

The truth was, Michael didn't. He'd lost his job and he seemed to be losing his father. Where was God in any of it? And even if God was around, what could he do about it? Michael never imagined God as a genie. Would he find Michael a job? And what about Pop—would God miraculously heal him from Alzheimer's? Probably not. Why would God do that for Pop when he didn't do it for the millions of other sufferers?

Michael didn't put any of these questions to Colleen. He didn't dare admit the darkness in his feelings. "You pray for us," he finally said.

She snuggled into the crook of his arm. He felt her arm move in the Sign of the Cross. She prayed softly. The words came from her heart as she appealed to the Blessed Virgin and various saints to pray to God on their behalf.

Michael thought of Clarence, who, if he kept his word, might be somewhere praying for him right now. Michael wondered if a multitude of voices might move God to action.

I can't count on that, Michael thought. *This is my problem to fix.*

Spooky Sally stopped by as they were about to leave for Hope Springs. Michael let out a soft groan as he saw her pull to the curb. Ethan and Madison immediately drifted away.

"I'm so glad I caught you," Sally said as she climbed out of her car. She was a heavyset woman who puffed and panted as she climbed the driveway, her red hair flying wildly around her face as if it had a weather system all its own. "You have to hear this!"

Colleen smiled pleasantly and invited her in for a *very quick* cup of coffee.

Michael was sorry that he'd already packed all the suitcases into the car. Standing with his hands in his pockets, he tried in vain to think of something else to do.

"Come on, Michael. You need to hear this," Sally said.

There was no escape.

They went into the kitchen. Colleen nodded her head for Michael to sit down.

Sally dropped into a chair and clasped her hands in front of her. She looked at Michael for a moment, her round face glowing from a source behind her bright red lipstick and heavy black mascara. He felt like she was about to ask for his palm to read his fortune. There was no other phrase for it, Michael thought . . . *she's spooky.*

"I had a picture last night while I was praying," she finally said, her eyes fixed on Michael. He knew from past experience that a *picture* for Sally meant a *vision*. "I saw you sitting in a small windowless room."

"Oh?" Colleen asked, trying to offset Michael's stony silence.

Sally kept her gaze on Michael. "You were at a table, carving a piece of wood. Directly in front of you was a heavy iron door."

"You've seen my office at work," Michael quipped.

Sally continued, "Then a key was pushed into the lock on the door. With heavy clicks and clanging and the sound of latches being drawn back, the door opened. Its rusty hinges groaned. Then a bright light poured in. You winced and covered your eyes. A figure stood framed in the doorway."

Michael glanced at Colleen. She looked captivated.

"The figure spoke to you," Sally went on. "He said, 'You promised to follow me. Will you follow me now?'"

Michael opened his mouth to speak, hoping to close the curtain on her picture.

"Wait!" Sally said, stifling him. "In my picture, you asked, 'Follow you to where?' And the figure said, 'To freedom.' You looked down at your carving and asked, 'What kind of freedom?' The figure said, 'Come and see.' She sat back and closed her eyes, exhaling as if she had just finished a critically acclaimed performance of Hamlet's *To be or not to be* soliloquy.

Michael opened his mouth to speak again, but this time Colleen laid a hand on his arm to stop him.

Sally sat forward, her green eyes wide. "You looked around at your cell and thought, *How can I leave this? I'm safe here. It has been my home for years.* And the light outside of the door was so bright that you couldn't see what was out there. You reasoned that maybe, just maybe, if you got a glimpse of what you were trading your cell for, then maybe, just maybe, you'd go.'"

Michael almost laughed. *She's a mind reader in her dreams*, he thought.

Sally continued, "So you asked, 'What is out there? Tell me and maybe I will go.' The figure receded, leaving only the light, and the door closed again. You went back to your carving as if nothing had happened. Then you forgot all about it."

Michael was alarmed to see that Sally's eyes had filled with tears. Big fat tears slid down her chin. She pulled a handkerchief from somewhere. "I haven't seen a sadder picture in all my years," she sniffed and blew her nose.

Leaning back, Michael folded his arms. "It's a little unsubtle for a vision, isn't it?"

"They're not *visions*," Sally said. "They're only pictures. And it isn't for me to say what it is or isn't. You need to figure that out for yourself."

"Okay, thanks," Michael said, making as if to stand up.

Sally reached for his hand and nearly pulled him across the table toward her. "Michael, please don't lock yourself in. Please don't stay in your cell."

Michael put on his best smile as he pulled his hand from hers. "I won't, Sally. Don't worry."

Hope Springs was a couple of hours' drive southwest of Denver, taking the Reynolds family into diverse landscapes of mountains, hills, and rolling fields with houses that looked like sets from a John Ford movie. Michael often looked at the vast landscape and imagined what had gone through the minds of the pioneers when they first approached from the East. Did they imagine their cabins and grazing cattle, or did they fear an unknown future fighting both nature and tribes of people who might not like their arrival?

The town had once been a gateway between a split in the sprawling Rocky Mountains. It was generally accepted that a U.S. Army captain named Richard Thorndyke discovered Hope Springs in the mid-1800s, when he explored the region with Professor John (Jack) Virtue, a scientist and self-proclaimed explorer. Allegedly, Professor Virtue named the area Hope Springs after a particularly grueling journey through the mountains. The caravan came upon the natural hot springs that would later become the biggest draw of the town. Thorndyke and Virtue set up a base camp. Pioneer families came later, as did treasure-seeking miners, the men who built the railroad, the women who worked as nurses in the hospitals, and many others who staked their claims to whatever the area might provide.

The hot springs became a major attraction as many came to be "healed" by the waters. A small sanitorium was built near the spring at the start of the twentieth century, later becoming a clinic and medical professional building right next to the Royal Hotel, which offered the hot springs as part of its attractions. A second hot springs was discovered in the mountains and was now part of the new Pine Creek Pass Resort, built near it.

Like many Colorado towns, Hope Springs had periods when it flourished and when it didn't. It was a "four-season" town that gave year-round reasons for tourists to visit: skiing, plenty of hiking, hunting and fishing, colorful aspens, and a quaint downtown with lots of shops and restaurants to enjoy.

For Michael, it was a good place to grow up, but not to live out his life. Once he was able to escape to college, he knew he would only ever return to visit. He worked hard to break free of what he considered a small-town mentality. Whenever he returned, he felt as if he'd entered a time warp and had been transported into a vortex that threatened to pull him back to his past. Hope Springs was, for him, a constant reminder of a life long gone. Memories walked like ghosts among the living.

"Just call me Marty McFly," he said to Colleen as they entered the city limits.

"Marty *who*?" Madison asked from the back seat.

Michael looked in the rearview mirror at his daughter. "*Back to the Future*?"

She shook her head.

"How can you *not* know a film so important to our culture?" he asked.

"*Your* culture," Madison said.

"If it's not on that Tip-Top app, then she won't see it," Ethan added.

They drove past neighborhoods of cozy houses, the mountains watching over them like the sacred giants they once had been. They drove through the downtown, noting which businesses were still there and which ones had been replaced. They lamented the loss of this locally owned business, or that one, and the increasing number of chain stores that had replaced them. Michael was pleased to see that the relatively new Hagan's Bookshop was still there and busy.

Michael saw Mrs. Emmerson, his First Communion teacher at St. Clare of Assisi Catholic Church. She was ancient then and, by all mathematical equations, should have died by now. But there she stood in the doorway of a shop, chatting amiably with another woman. "Straighten your tie," he could hear her saying with a breath that smelled of lozenges and a smile that came from dentures that seemed too big. The boys in the class had a yearlong debate about whether or not she wore a wig until Tony Santino confessed that he'd once seen the wig blown clean off her head by a gust of wind. "She's *bald*!" Tony had gasped.

And how could he drive past Rudy's Tastee-Whiz without seeing old Mr. Rudy, white paper cap on his head and stained apron around his waist, standing like a master chef at the green-and-chrome milkshake maker?

But Michael knew Old Mr. Rudy had been dead for years, and the recipe for the best chocolate shakes in the world went to the grave with him. The Tastee-Whiz was now a taco shack.

As they slowly drove down Main Street, Michael envisioned his deceased mother as a young woman. She appeared everywhere: standing in line at Greene's Grocery with its front tent flaps and the smell of vegetables heavy with the moisture of a sprinkler system that sprayed produce and customers at random ... walking into Kendall's Pharmacy ... waiting to get tickets for a show at the Coliseum Cinema ... strolling down the street from Hayes Department Store, shopping bag on her arm, her face young and her hair tucked under a floppy hat.

Michael described all of this to his family. Colleen mentioned ghosts of her own. She also saw Michael's mother, but as an older woman, the one who became a loving mother-in-law and a doting grandmother. She appeared to Colleen as they drove past the fountain in front of City Hall where, on more than one occasion, she had chased little Ethan and given ice cream to baby Madison.

Ethan said he saw ghosts of old family members near the pavilion behind Hope Springs High School, where they had gathered once a year for the big family reunion with distant relatives whose names he could never remember. Ethan saw them all now as he'd seen them then, leaning over red-checkered picnic tables piled with fried chicken, potato salad, corn, and home-baked bread that was still warm. There they were—pitching horseshoes and sitting on lawn chairs under the trees. And at nightfall, when everything was being packed up, Ethan and his cousins caught lightning bugs that winked at them with little green lights and put them in empty jars with holes in the tops.

For Madison, the only ghost was her grandfather, though a younger version of the one she knew she would see today. His ghost had a slender, unwrinkled face and hair that winged over his ears. She remembered him sitting in his favorite chair, making faces at her and reading her a story. He had shown her how to color within the lines by tracing everything in black first. He had taught her to play Chinese checkers. He had given her rides on his back, prancing and bucking like a rodeo horse. Together they sat at the old player piano down in the basement, even though she was more interested in the various levers and the way the piano keys moved by themselves than the music it played. (The piano was gone, she knew ... sold to an antique shop for next to nothing.) And as the sun would set, they'd sit on an old-fashioned metal glider on the porch, sliding back and forth, back and forth. The howls of coyotes and the cries of foxes came from somewhere in the dark beyond the pines. One night they watched a bobcat slink across the yard, probably in search of one of the rabbits that inhabited the area.

Three of the Reynolds family said they welcomed the memories and the pleasure they brought. Michael alone did not say so. His memories brought with them a feeling that Michael couldn't identify—something both bittersweet and uncomfortable.

Hope Springs represented the passage of time, to be sure, and, with it, a nostalgia of days he'd never see again. It reminded him of the slow march everyone was making. And with that reminder came a longing for something he doubted he could ever fulfill, especially since he didn't know what it was.

He shrugged the feelings off. Going back to carefree days or happier times never solved any of today's problems. The world spun on indifferently. He was unemployed and his father might have Alzheimer's disease, and nothing in his memories of Hope Springs could do anything about either problem.

* * *

Pop's place sat on the corner of Braddock and Charles Streets in the "Old Federal" section of town—so-named because of the federal money that had built the houses right after World War II. Most of them were boxy and cramped, but Pop had scored a model that was expanded by the original owner, an architect. It still had white vinyl siding and a black-shingled roof; a narrow brick chimney framed one side. A windmill stood in the middle of the front garden, and a very politically incorrect figurine of a black stable boy in a red shirt and white pants held a lantern by the front door. Untrimmed bushes threatened to rise above the windows lining the front and sides. A large pine tree cast its shade over one corner of the house. The entire plot of land was encased by a short white picket fence that now leered at them like broken teeth.

"Something else to fix," Michael said as they pulled into the driveway. He brought the car to a stop behind Pop's old Dodge, which sat halfway in and halfway out of the freestanding garage. There was a scrape along the rear right fender.

"Is he going to be different?" Madison asked from the back seat.

"I don't know," Michael said. It was the first time either of his children had seemed worried.

Colleen half-turned in her seat. "He probably won't look different, but he may act different. Be patient. Don't argue. Just treat him with the same love and respect you always have."

Dead leaves lay scattered around the front porch, the cold breeze gently prodding them to the corners and under the rusting metal rocking chair. The glass on the storm door was gone, leaving just the frame. The inside door was open.

Michael gave the wall a sharp knock. "Pop!" Michael called out, slowly stepping in. "It's a little cold to leave the door open, isn't it?"

Colleen followed and sniffed the air. "It smells like he burned something in the kitchen." She continued on through the living room and the dining room, disappearing into the kitchen.

Michael surveyed the living room and the unusual clutter that filled it. Pop was an Arabian merchant at heart, Michael often thought. He bought things he didn't need just in case someone he knew might want one. The junk—things like old radios and Philco televisions and hooded hairdryers and record players—were usually kept in the basement and brought in or taken out through the double doors that once serviced the coal wagons. Now the clutter had moved upstairs. Three tube televisions of various sizes now sat along one wall. An old Underwood typewriter covered an end table, displacing a lamp to the floor. The coffee table was overflowing with small boxes, some containing bits of machinery or sections of pipe.

"And you complain about *my* room," Ethan said.

From the kitchen Colleen cried out.

"What's wrong?" Michael called to her.

She appeared around the corner. "I'm going to have to buy some rubber gloves and give this place a *deep* clean. You can't see the sink for the dishes."

"Pop!" Michael called out again. There was no answer.

"I'll see if he's upstairs," Madison said and dashed away to the staircase.

Michael folded his arms and clenched his fists under his armpits. "This was a mistake. We should have told Aunt Minnie to bring Pop to us for his birthday. This town, this house, makes me feel like I've walked face-first into a giant cobweb."

"Gripe, gripe, gripe," Ethan teased. "I don't think there's anything wrong with this town or this house." He dropped on the couch, then instantly hiked his butt up. He felt underneath and retrieved an original Ping-Pong paddle. "Does Pop have a Ping-Pong table?"

"Not for years."

"He must be out," Madison said as she bounded back down the stairs.

Michael wondered if he should check the basement.

"Can we go shopping later?" Madison asked as she slung herself over the arm of a chair. "I want to see if they've opened any tattoo parlors."

Michael shot her a warning glance.

"Aunt Minnie said they've opened a new natural foods shop," Colleen said from the kitchen.

"Then what are we waiting for?" Ethan asked with feigned excitement.

"Did you see all the signs for the funeral homes on the way in? I never noticed so many before," Madison said.

"Maybe that's a business you should get into," Ethan suggested to his father. "Do something new. Golden arches and a drive-up window for the viewing."

"I think it's already been done," Michael said.

Colleen reappeared in the doorway with an open can of dog food in one hand and a bottle of floor wax in the other. "Why do you think these were in the refrigerator?"

"Does he have a dog?" Madison asked.

"I don't think so," her dad replied.

Madison jumped up and began to search the house, making dog-calling noises.

"I found an old green pillow in the cupboard," Colleen said. "Then I realized it used to be a loaf of white bread."

Michael spread his arms to the room. "What are we going to do with all this junk? No nursing home will allow it."

"As if you'll ever get him to go to one," Ethan said. He brightened and asked, "Why not ask him to come live with us?"

Michael shook his head. "If what Aunt Minnie says is right, he'll need professional care. And we'll be living in a refrigerator box in the park if I don't find a job."

Colleen emerged from the kitchen with a worried look on her face. "We don't have to talk about this right now. We're here for his birthday. We're going to dress up in costumes, have cake and ice cream, and make a night of it. It'll be a nice celebration. We can deal with all the serious things afterward."

Michael held up a hand. "Wait a minute. Costumes? What costumes?"

"It was Aunt Minnie's idea," Colleen said. "We thought we could dig through the boxes in the attic and dress up. You know how your father loved that sort of thing."

"My father loves that sort of thing so he can laugh at how ridiculous people look," Michael said.

Colleen frowned at him. "Michael, we didn't drive all this way to brood or argue. We're going to celebrate his birthday however he wants. It's not every day that a man has his eightieth birthday. It's a milestone."

Millstone, Michael thought.

Madison drifted down the stairs. "No dog," she announced. "But if you think this room is bad, just wait until you see the rest of them."

———————————◆———————————

There were four bedrooms on the second floor: the master, Michael's old room, Dennis's, and a guest room. The attic had been converted into a fifth bedroom for Ethan and Madison to use when they were smaller, or Dennis's kids, depending on who was visiting. They were now filled with more clutter—stacks of newspapers and magazines, a collection of Zane Grey books that had never made it to any bookshelf, and various table lamps.

Ethan now claimed the attic for himself but would have to clear aside the various vintage telephones, food mixers, a console record

player, and an oversized rear-projection television. Madison went
into what had once been her father's room, which seemed mostly
untouched with its mementos of his young life there. Michael and
Colleen put their things in the guest room. It was now filled with
old radios, stereos, and shaving kits from an old barber shop. A
mustiness filled the air.

Colleen began to unpack their clothes and put them in a tall
chest of drawers.

Michael sat down on the bed. The springs rattled and scraped.
"How are we going to clean out this place?"

"Why worry about it?" she asked. "Pop will never let you do it."

"He'll have no choice if we have to move him into a retirement
place," Michael said. "We'll have to clean it up to sell it."

Colleen gave him a doubtful look. Then she asked, "What if we
don't sell it?"

Michael gazed at her. What could she possibly be thinking? Then
he remembered what Spooky Sally had said. "Forget about that.
We're not living here."

She handed him a couple of shirts to hang up. The closet smelled
of mothballs. The garment rack wobbled as if it might come loose
from the wall. A square hinged door was cut into the floor. It
covered a laundry chute to the basement. Michael remembered
that Dennis had fallen down that chute when he was eight. His
fall was broken by a pile of laundry that had gathered at the
bottom. Dennis had a few scratches and bumps. Pop then covered
all of the laundry chutes in the house. That didn't stop Michael
from imagining monsters crawling up to the square doors—and
scratching to get in.

Michael glanced at his watch. They'd been there half an hour
and still no sign of Pop. Should he be worried? Didn't Alzheimer's

sufferers often go strolling off on a simple errand and then forget who they were and where they lived? Michael looked over at Colleen. He could tell by her face that she was thinking the same thing.

"I'll call Aunt Minnie," Colleen said lightly, as if she wanted to talk about the party. But Michael knew better.

Aunt Minnie's phone rang and rang. Colleen put the phone handset back on the cradle. Michael was leaning against the wall in the kitchen. He was about to suggest they call the police, but then the front door opened and in walked Pop and Aunt Minnie. They were carrying grocery bags.

"What is this, a home invasion?" Pop called out.

"I hope so. Take all the spoils you can," Aunt Minnie said.

"We were getting worried," Michael said to Aunt Minnie as he took the bags from her.

She kissed him on the cheek. "It's good to see you, too."

She smelled of a perfume she'd been wearing for years. Though she had a few years on Pop, she looked younger, mostly due to her natural good health and her sharp fashion sense. No old-people's clothes for her. But what always startled Michael were her eyes—sharp and knowing—and they made him think of his mother.

"You look like a million," he said to her.

She poked a playful finger at him. "I'm only eighty-two. Don't push it."

Michael took the bags of groceries into the kitchen and sat them on the small Formica and metal table Pop used for breakfast. It had two matching metal chairs with red pads on the backs and seats. The pads were cracked and split. Colleen got busy putting groceries away.

Pop stood in front of the open refrigerator trying to figure out where to put a jar of pickles. The shelves were full.

"Leave it to me," Colleen said, taking the jar away from him. "I'll get this sorted out."

"Sorted?" he asked.

"A few things are long past their expiration dates," Colleen said.

"Expiration dates are for cowards," Pop said. He surveyed the kitchen. "Did you clean up in here? Now I'll never find anything."

"Just ask the cockroaches," Michael said.

Pop wagged a finger at him. "I don't have those. Clutter doesn't mean unhygienic," he said.

The sounds of Minnie greeting Ethan and Madison in the living room caught Pop's attention. "I haven't said hello to the kids." He drifted away.

Colleen said to Michael, "Most of what's in the refrigerator will have to be thrown away. Honestly, there are a few brands in there that went out of business before the turn of the century."

"Which century?" Michael asked.

She gently pushed him to the door. "Go on. I have to do this on my own."

"I'll rent you a hazmat suit," he said.

In the living room, Pop was clearing things off of chairs that Michael hadn't realized were chairs at all. "Everybody, sit down."

"We're going to give this whole house a good cleaning before we leave," Michael announced.

"What's wrong with this house?" Pop asked. "There's *nothing* wrong with it."

"That's what I keep telling him," Ethan said.

Michael frowned at his son. "I'm not surprised you'd think so. You inherited a natural instinct for clutter from your grandfather. But instead of old televisions, you've collected old computers."

"And that's a problem *why*?" Ethan asked.

"I'm waiting for us to get cited for radiation leaks from all those old tubes," Michael said.

"You're a perfectionist," Ethan said. "Who did you inherit *that* from?"

"No one in this family," Pop said. He stood, slightly hunched, and rubbed his hand thoughtfully across his chin. Michael noticed that he'd missed a patch of stubble near his left ear. "Though come to think of it, I had a cousin, John, who was a perfectionist. He covered everything in plastic to keep it clean—the couches and chairs, the tables, the kids ..."

"They all had respiratory problems," Aunt Minnie said.

Pop continued, "A place for everything, and everything in its place. That's what John always said. No one in the family liked him. He always smelled of Pine-Sol, like someone had dumped hand sanitizer on a Christmas tree. He wasn't right in the head. They say his mother gave him too much soy milk when he was growing up."

"I'm not a perfectionist," Michael protested to Ethan. "Technically, a perfectionist is someone who cannot accept anything short of perfection. I've spent my whole life accepting mediocrity." He paused, realizing what he'd just said as his two kids looked at him. "I mean, uh ..."

Aunt Minnie bailed him out. "There's nothing wrong with a little bit of clutter. Just so it's clean clutter."

"And that's the magic word, Ethan," Michael said, trying to recover the moment. "*Clean.* Your haven't-been-washed-in-three-months gym socks don't qualify. Late at night I can hear them kicking at your bedroom door, trying to get out."

Ethan smirked at his father.

"I wish I had a reason to wear gym socks," Aunt Minnie said. "All I get to wear are orthopedic odor-eaters. But they put a sporty racing stripe on the sides to make me feel active."

With a soft grunt, Pop dropped into his favorite chair. Michael watched him, trying to notice some change, any proof of what Aunt Minnie had told them in her letter. He looked the same as he always did: his ready smile, twinkling eyes, and thin strands of gray hair adorning his otherwise bald top. *Were those brown age spots just above his forehead?* Michael couldn't tell. He wore faded brown polyester trousers and a blue-and-white checked flannel shirt.

He's dressing like an old man, Michael thought. Had he always, or was Michael only now noticing it for the first time? "How are you feeling, Dad?" Michael asked.

"Never felt better."

Michael looked at him, surprised. "Really?"

"Well, I *did* feel better one weekend in 1967."

"What happened in 1967?" Ethan asked.

"I have no idea," Pop said. "Do you remember 1967, Minnie?"

Minnie was indignant. "I was a mere child."

Pop turned his attention to Madison. "You're growing up fast. Cut it out or you'll be hitting your head on chandeliers."

Madison grinned at him. It was something he always said to her.

"Well, boy, how's school?" Pop asked Ethan. "It's your last year, right?"

"First year," Ethan said. "First *semester*, I should say."

Pop suddenly jabbed a finger at Ethan's goatee. "You smeared chocolate on your face."

Ethan touched his chin self-consciously.

Pop chuckled. "Did you hear about the man who grew his beard so long that one day, when he was running for the bus, he tripped on it and ran all the way up to his chin."

Ethan laughed politely. Michael knew his kids had heard Pop tell that joke dozens of times before.

"Got enough money?" Pop asked and reached for his wallet.

"No, Dad. We're fine," Michael said quickly.

Pop said, "You were let go. Isn't that right? I had to hear it from Minnie. You could have told me yourself."

Michael shot a disapproving look to Aunt Minnie. She looked contrite. "I'll give Colleen a hand in the kitchen," she said.

At that moment, Colleen rounded the corner, wiping her hands on a dish towel.

"How many years were you with the company?" Pop asked Michael.

"Thirty-something. I don't want to talk about it."

Pop shook his head. "That's the difference between a company and a corporation. Companies think in terms of keeping company with people. Corporations think in terms of keeping ... uh ..." Pop struggled, looking as if he'd gotten lost in his own thought.

"Corpses?" Ethan offered.

Pop looked at Ethan with an uncomprehending expression.

"A career change is good for a man your age," Aunt Minnie said. "Just today, I was thinking about applying for a job as a yoga instructor. Just imagine those stretchy pants over my adult diapers."

"Ew," Madison said.

"We have to talk seriously about this," Pop said to Michael. "You have bills to pay."

"I know, Dad," Michael said.

"How're you going to afford to keep Ethan in school?" Pop asked.

"Or buy me a belly button ring?" Madison added.

Pop started to dig into his pocket. "I've got money here somewhere." He shifted this way and that, trying to find his wallet. "I know I had my wallet a minute ago."

"It's probably on the seat in the car," Aunt Minnie said.

"Forget it, Dad. You're not going to cover anyone's tuition with what you've got in your wallet. A few dollars and some old business cards won't do it."

Pop frowned at him. "Spending money, then. I want to do *something*. I've been watching college football games. Those coed girls are mighty cute." He winked at Ethan.

"TV makes everyone look better," Ethan said. "All the coeds I know have thick glasses, crooked teeth, and stringy hair."

"You must be hanging around the English department," Pop said.

"Watch it, buster. *I* was an English major," Aunt Minnie said.

"My point exactly." Pop leaned forward in his chair. "Now, Ethan, you make sure to date while you're in college. That's how I met your grandmother. She was working in the library at the university and I was—"

"Here we go again." Michael rolled his eyes. It was a story they'd all heard a million times and could repeat by heart.

"Don't interrupt," Pop said. "She was working in the library at the university and I was ..." Pop stopped himself and looked confused. "I was doing something. What was I doing? Help me, Minnie. She was your sister."

"How should I know? It's your memory," she said.

"You were sisters," Pop said. "Sisters talk about those sorts of things."

"We only talked about the *good-looking* boys," Aunt Minnie said with a wry smile. She sat down next to Madison on the couch. "The only thing she said was that you kept annoying her at the library."

Pop nodded. "I kept making noise to get her attention."

"You almost got her fired," Aunt Minnie said.

Pop smiled. "A small sacrifice for love."

"A small sacrifice for you, maybe," Aunt Minnie countered. "You had nothing to lose."

"Yet I was willing to give it all up for her," Pop said. "You were jealous because I didn't ask *you* out."

Aunt Minnie barked out a loud "Ha!"

Pop gestured with a great flourish. "I stood on the library steps and sang her a song when she came out. It was a regular serenade on my accordion. I'll never forget it."

"It was a ukulele," Aunt Minnie corrected him.

"No, it was a harmonica. And I—" Pop stopped again, a shadow crossing his face. "I—"

He clearly couldn't remember what he was about to say.

Michael looked to Aunt Minnie for help.

"The point your grandfather is trying to make," Aunt Minnie said calmly to Ethan, taking attention away from Pop, "is that you get yourself to a good college so you can meet a woman like your grandmother."

Pop nodded. "That's right. You don't need an education when you have a woman like that. And if you can't find one like her, then look for one like your aunt Minnie here. In the English department."

"I will—*if* I go back to college," Ethan said.

"Now, Ethan—" Michael began.

Colleen stepped forward and put a hand on his shoulder. She spoke quickly. "I think that's enough reminiscing for now."

"Do you have a dog?" Madison asked Pop.

"A dog? No, why?"

Colleen gave Madison a sharp look.

"Because we were thinking of getting you one for your birthday," Madison said. "Which reminds me: happy birthday!" She went to him and kissed him on the cheek.

"*Is* it my birthday?" Pop said. "Easy to forget when there are no *presents* around to remind me."

Colleen patted him on the arm. "Be patient."

"Did you all eat? Are you hungry? I made some stew," said Pop with a brisk rubbing of his hands.

"We had a big breakfast," Michael told him.

Pop looked at his watch. "But it's two fifteen. You must be starving."

"It's ten 'til twelve," Ethan said.

"That's Denver time. It'll only take a minute to warm up." Pop climbed out of the chair and hustled off to the kitchen.

"His watch has been stopped at two fifteen for three weeks," Aunt Minnie informed them quietly.

Madison whispered, "I hope he isn't going to make the stew out of that dog food."

"I threw that away," Colleen said.

Michael gestured for Aunt Minnie to come out to the front porch. "We need to talk," he said.

Michael shoved his hands in his pockets and leaned back against the wooden rail of the porch. Aunt Minnie sat on an old rocker. Colleen sat on the edge of a metal deck chair. A brisk breeze blew through. The women shivered and hugged themselves.

"Well?" Aunt Minnie asked.

"He *looks* good," Colleen said, pleased. "The way you talked on the phone, I expected—"

Aunt Minnie held up a hand, glancing back at the door as if she feared Pop might walk through. She said, "We went to the doctor's this morning. That's why we were late."

"Dr. Janssen?" Michael asked.

Aunt Minnie shook her head. "No. A specialist Dr. Janssen wanted Pop to see. Dr. Collins. A neuropsychiatrist." Aunt Minnie looked out toward the street and for a moment Michael saw the age in her face. "It was all I could do to get him there. Finally I had to tell him we were going so that *I* could get a check-up."

"So, what happened?" Michael asked.

"He was furious that the doctor was for him," Aunt Minnie said. "He would've walked out if I hadn't blackmailed him."

"How did you do that?" Colleen asked.

"I told him that I would call and tell you not to come visit if he didn't cooperate. So he stayed."

"Then what?" asked Michael.

"Dr. Collins went over all of Dr. Janssen's notes about your father, his health history, lab results, changes in his behavior and personality ... I hardly know what all there was. Then he gave your father a bunch of cognitive tests. The kind to check his memory, his problem-solving abilities, counting ... and he took some blood and urine."

"Dad put up with all of that?" Michael asked.

"Not happily," Aunt Minnie said. "Dr. Collins wants more specific tests—brain scans and such. He wants to refer him to a geriatric doctor and neurologist. But your father hit his limit and said it's a lot of fuss about nothing. And that was it."

"So, there's no diagnosis?" Colleen asked.

Minnie tipped her head just a little, as if she was listening to something from somewhere. Michael realized she was allowing the sun to warm her face for a moment. Then she said, "Dr. Collins told me privately that he's pretty sure your father has Alzheimer's disease. And, from my point of view, it's getting worse all the time."

"How is it getting worse?" Colleen asked. "Your letter didn't have a lot of details except that he keeps losing things and nearly fell down the stairs."

"The details are small, everyday kinds of things. Little things. On their own, they seem like normal aging problems ..." Aunt Minnie's voice trailed off.

"What 'little things'?" Michael asked. "I didn't think nearly falling down the stairs was a 'little thing.' What other kinds of little things are there?"

Aunt Minnie sighed. "I don't know where to begin. Did you notice his shoes?"

"His shoes." Michael repeated it, trying to think if he'd noticed them.

"He was wearing slip-ons," Colleen remembered.

Michael was surprised. His father hated slip-ons. He called them "sissy shoes." Michael had bought him a pair for Christmas one year and, as far as he knew, Pop never wore them. He searched Aunt Minnie's face for what it meant.

Aunt Minnie swallowed hard and told the story in a soft voice that trembled ever so slightly. "One afternoon a couple of weeks ago I came over and he was sitting in his chair. Just sitting. He looked like he'd been crying. At first I thought he'd been thinking about Linda ... he's been doing that a lot lately. Reminiscing a lot about your mother. I guess that's one of the things that happens. With Alzheimer's, I mean. People spend more time in the past, and they get more emotional. But he wasn't crying about your mother. He was crying because he forgot how to tie his shoes."

Michael was stunned. Colleen lowered her head.

Aunt Minnie dabbed at her nose with a tissue that seemed to appear from nowhere. "If you look in his closet, you'll find a couple pairs of slip-on shoes, and those sneakers with the Velcro straps."

Michael watched her. From her look, there was more to be said. "Did you find the can of dog food?" she asked.

"Yes," said Colleen.

"You'll find more in the pantry."

"Why did he buy dog food?" Colleen asked.

"Because he was convinced that he had a dog," Aunt Minnie replied. "Worse, he was scared to death that he hadn't fed the poor thing for days and days. He ran out and bought a dozen cans of food. He even put some in a bowl and left it on the floor. I threw it away one day when I was trying to tidy up."

"Where did he get the idea that he had a dog?" Michael asked.

Aunt Minnie shook her head. "Where do any of these ideas come from? It's like he falls into a dream." She wrung the tissue in her fingers. "One morning Bill McKendricks found your dad out front trying to shovel snow off the driveway. He was in his bathrobe, and barefooted."

"Had it been snowing?" Colleen asked.

"No," Aunt Minnie said. "Needless to say, it caused quite a stir in the neighborhood."

Michael began to pace around the porch.

"I caught him one morning as he was heading out the door for work," Aunt Minnie went on. "He was wearing a pair of overalls and his old miner's cap. He was headed for the mines."

Colleen sat back on the metal glider. It made scraping, rusty noises. "He hasn't worked at the mines since he was a teenager, right?"

"Right," Aunt Minnie said.

Michael rubbed his chin as he tried to sort through what Aunt Minnie was saying. "Is that enough to have him put in a home?" he asked, already knowing the answer.

Aunt Minnie leveled her gaze at Michael. "Apart from doing something dangerous, or hurting himself, he's also having accidents."

"Accidents?" Michael asked.

"You mean incontinence," Colleen said.

"He's losing control of his body." Aunt Minnie dabbed at her eyes again.

Michael leaned against the porch rail. *My father is in diapers*, he thought.

"His forgetfulness is chronic," Aunt Minnie said. "One evening I came around to find he hadn't eaten all day. He insisted he had, but I could tell he hadn't. When I tried to fix him something, he kept protesting that he'd eaten only a few minutes ago, and I knew full well that he was wrong. After I fed him and cleared the plates away, he wanted to know when it was time to eat because he was starving."

"This must be awful for you," Colleen said softly.

"I wish you had told us sooner," said Michael. He felt bad for his aunt. She had stepped up to care for Pop in saintly ways after his mother had died. Now he felt guilty for not coming to visit more often.

"I didn't know what to say," Aunt Minnie replied, tears coming to her eyes. "Everything was spread out over time, so I didn't think it was anything but old age catching up to him. But now I feel terrible for not realizing sooner. And I feel awful because I can't take care of him. Not the way he needs. And there are the other feelings I get. Feelings I'm ashamed of."

"What kinds of feelings?" Colleen asked.

"Hurt, mostly. Anger sometimes," she said. "He accused me of stealing his pen. It wasn't even a special pen, just something he'd picked up somewhere. But he couldn't find it and he called me in a rage. He said I was a thief. I told him I didn't have his pen, that he'd probably misplaced it, but then he called me a liar and hung up. I almost stopped speaking to him altogether for that. Then he called me to complain that the neighbors were sneaking into the house and stealing his belongings. Nobody had stolen anything. He'd simply misplaced them."

Michael sighed.

"I'd lose my patience," Aunt Minnie continued. "He'd call to say the television was broken for the tenth time. I'd come over to find out that he'd been sitting on the remote control. Or he'd push random buttons until the TV was so confused that it simply shut down. One day he had somehow changed the cable box to *Korean*. I had to get my nephew over to put it back to English. It goes on and on."

"How did you get him to Dr. Janssen?" Colleen asked.

"I waited for the panic."

"What panic?"

"The few moments when he would admit that something was wrong. He'd get a particular look in his eyes, like he was horribly confused. That's when he would agree to see the doctor. You'll want to watch for those times." She sniffled and blew her nose.

A low rumbling sound came from somewhere in the house.

Madison appeared at the screen door, her face a mosaic through the mesh. "You better come in."

The rumbling came from under the floor. Michael walked to the kitchen where it was the loudest. He rounded the corner and saw Ethan sitting at the small table. Ethan's shoe was off. He was rubbing his foot. He gave Michael a helpless look.

Pop was standing at the sink. The cabinet doors underneath were standing open. Pop was trying to kick at the pipes.

"What in the—?" Michael began to say.

"It's all right," Pop said. "It's the pipes under the sink. They make a racket and you have to kick them."

"I tried," Ethan said.

"You've got to do it a certain way," Pop chided him. He gave the P-trap a hard kick.

Michael imagined the pipe breaking free. He stepped forward to stop his father. But the rumbling suddenly stopped.

"See?" Pop said.

"You should get those pipes fixed, Dad," said Michael.

"I'm used to them."

Michael turned to Ethan. "Are you all right?"

Ethan wiggled his toes. "I think my career in the ballet is over."

"Think we can get any money for your old tutus?" Michael asked.

Pop called out. "To the dining room table. Everybody, sit down, eat some stew." He slipped on some threadbare oven mitts and grabbed a bubbling pot from the stove.

Colleen appeared and, with more hands than she actually had, grabbed bowls and silverware and laid them onto the dining table. She handed Pop a ladle.

"Sit down," Pop said, dropping a mitt onto the table and placing the pot top. "Come on, Minnie."

Aunt Minnie shook her head. "I can't stay. I've got to run."

"Why? What's the rush?" He looked at his watch. "It's only two fifteen."

"I'm getting you a new watch, Dad."

"I don't need a new watch; this one works fine." Pop began to stir the stew. "Why are you running off, Minnie?"

"I'm taking Val Swenson to the hairdresser's," Aunt Minnie said.

"The hairdresser! Again?" Pop said. "I swear, she's got it a different color every time I see her. I'm going to start calling her 'Technicolor.'"

"Well, she isn't Technicolor now. She got caught in an automatic sprinkler system and all the color rinsed out."

Pop grunted. "I don't know why women fuss with their hair so much. They should leave the color alone. Leave it natural, the way God intended. Who cares if it turns gray? I don't. The whitened hair of the elderly is a crown; isn't that what the Bible says?"

"I don't know," Aunt Minnie replied. "I wasn't there when it was written."

Pop shook his head. "I'm not ashamed of being old. Eighty years is something to be proud of. Don't you think?"

Everyone mumbled their agreements. Madison had joined the gathering around the table. They all stood, looking unsure of what to do. Michael watched his father curiously. Something was happening that he couldn't remember ever seeing before.

Pop's tone got darker and angrier. A redness appeared on his ears and spread to his cheeks. "You tell those people at the church! There's nothing wrong with growing old. Tell them! I'm not too old to teach a catechism class. Who are they to tell me I can't do it anymore? I can do it. I've been a good teacher. Over fifty years at that church, teaching those kids, and they say I can't—" Pop stopped himself. He looked at each one of them. "Why are you just standing around? Eat your stew!"

Colleen moved in next to him and took the ladle from his hand. "Sit down. I'll serve."

Pop dropped into the chair at the end of the table.

Ethan stepped over and began to hand the filled bowls around.

Madison, her eyes never leaving her grandfather, sat down and pulled a bowl toward her.

Aunt Minnie quietly turned and walked to the front door. Michael followed her.

"What was all that?" Michael asked Aunt Minnie quietly.

Aunt Minnie grabbed her coat from the coat stand. Michael helped her into it. She said, "Father Cliff politely asked your father to step aside from teaching. It's ... he hasn't ..."

"Stop whispering at the front door!" Pop shouted from the dining room.

Aunt Minnie strode back to the dining room. "Don't worry about it, James. You've been a good teacher. Bob Simpson said he became a priest because of your teaching and he's working in South America as a missionary. And who knows who else you've inspired ..." She struggled for words. "None of us will know the kind of influence you've had until we gather in Heaven, but ... well, don't let it poison you. Father Cliff didn't mean anything by it."

Pop sat pouting with his arms folded across his chest. "I lose my place and ramble a bit. Younger folks do it and no one thinks anything." He lapsed into a brooding silence.

Aunt Minnie looked at Michael and Colleen with a sympathetic expression. Then she leaned between Ethan and Madison and whispered, "Don't take it personally. He's not doing any of this on purpose."

"You're whispering again," Pop said.

Aunt Minnie gave the two kids a quick kiss on the cheek and walked out.

They all sat down to a silence that was thicker than Pop's stew. Michael took a few bites and was relieved that it didn't taste like dog food.

Pop pushed his bowl away. "I'm not hungry," he said. "I'm going up to my room."

The Reynolds family looked at each other as Pop pushed his chair back and marched out. They heard him stomp up the stairs.

"I'll go up." Michael shoved another spoonful of the stew into his mouth and stood up.

"*Please* don't talk to him about anything important," Colleen said. "Wait until after the party."

"What difference will it make?" Michael asked.

"Maybe it won't. So, you may as well wait," she said.

Michael made no promises.

The door to Pop's bedroom was open. Michael could see Pop lying on his bed. He wasn't sleeping. A Zane Grey paperback was propped up on his chest.

Michael could have been fifteen again and the scene would have been the same. He saw his mother sitting across the room at her vanity, brushing her long brown hair. Then he saw her standing at the oak wardrobe, choosing a dress. Then she was over at the tallboy, putting fresh laundry away. She turned and smiled at Michael.

He blinked and she was gone. But the room was the same. His father hadn't changed anything in it since his mother's death. The only difference was the ever-encroaching clutter and a gray layer of dust.

"Dad?"

Pop didn't move, but said, "Nobody understands. Nobody could possibly understand." Then, with an audible effort, Pop put the book aside and sat up.

"I want to understand, Dad."

"You can't."

Michael sat on the edge of the bed. "Try. Tell me what's happening to you."

Pop's voice was nearly a whisper. "I don't know why I got so upset." He squirmed. "It feels like everyone is ganging up on me."

"What do you mean?" Michael asked.

Pop slowly lowered his head. "I forget things. Little things that I've known all my life. It's so ... frustrating. I forget words. I have some days when I can't put my thoughts together. The other day I was talking to Dale Johnson across the street. I wanted to tell him about the petunias growing in the back yard. But I couldn't think of the word. That word."

"Petunias? A lot of people would forget what they're called."

"I forgot the word *yard*. I stood there stumbling and stammering like a fool."

Michael patted his father's leg. "*Yard* is an easy word to forget, Dad. I forget it all the time. Mine hasn't been mowed in months."

"Don't patronize me," Pop said and rubbed his eyes. "I know why you're here. And don't say it's for my birthday. Minnie told you about the doctor. That woman is incapable of keeping a secret."

"It shouldn't be a secret, Dad. Why would you keep secrets from us?"

"The same reason you do. Why didn't you tell me you lost your job?"

"Let's keep this conversation focused on you right now," Michael said, not wanting to get sidetracked.

"I don't want to talk about me." He started digging in his trouser pockets for his wallet again. "You need money, don't you? How much do you need?"

"I don't need money, Dad. I told you before."

"It's a dirty trick laying a man off after he's been there so many years. You're a good worker, Michael. I know it. You were always the conscientious one. Responsible. Everything was neat and orderly for you. And I've been proud of you, son. Good wife. Fine grandchildren. I've been proud."

Michael looked at his father, wondering if this outpouring was sincere or another symptom.

Pop looked at Michael anxiously, his voice pleading. "You see? I'm talking and I'm not forgetting any of the words. I'm not angry anymore, either. I'll quit teaching the class at church if that's what they want me to do. Father Cliff knows what's best. He's always been a good friend." He held out his wallet again. "How much do you need?"

Michael realized that his father was ducking and dodging the real subject. "We need to talk about your future, Dad."

"There's nothing to talk about," Pop said. "Minnie shouldn't have told you anything. The doctors are drawing the wrong conclusions."

"Are they?"

Pop clenched his lips together until they were thin white strips.

"Dad?"

Then he blurted it out. "Minnie thinks I should move. Can you believe it? She wants me to move out of this house."

"She's worried," Michael explained. "We all are."

"I don't need anyone to take care of me," Pop said. "I won't sell this house. It's *my* house. I'm fine, Michael. I just have moments. Everyone has moments."

"Dad—"

"I'm eighty years old. I'm showing some signs of my age. Let's see how *you* are when you're eighty."

"I hope you're around for that," Michael said. He tried to sound reasonable, practical. "But I don't see how you can stay here alone—"

Pop shook his head defiantly. "It's in my will, Michael. You'll get it when I die. Not before."

"I don't want the house." Michael could feel the tension in his tone.

Pop folded his arms. "I'm not sick."

"You're not?" Michael leapt from the bed and went to the closet. He pushed open the door and confirmed what Aunt Minnie had told him. "Look at your shoes, Dad. Why are you wearing shoes without laces?"

Pop shrugged. "It's the latest style. I read it in *People* magazine."

"Shoveling snow when it hasn't snowed—is that the latest style, too?" Michael asked.

"I'll have to look in *People*." He spread his arms. "I wasn't feeling well. I was sleepwalking. You used to sleepwalk, too, and I didn't ask you to sell your house."

"Come on, Dad. What'll be next—playing jacks in the middle of Main Street? Or maybe you'll go wandering off completely and I'll have to send out an Amber Alert on everyone's phones."

"I don't even know what that means."

"I'm trying to be reasonable."

"You're not doing a very good job of it," Pop said, goading him.

Michael knew it was a losing battle. "All right. Never mind. We'll talk about this later."

"We won't talk about this *ever*," Pop said, his voice shaking. "All that I have is in this house and you want me to leave it. Where will I go? Where will you put me? Some hole in Denver? One of those nursing homes?"

Michael moved toward the door. "Never mind, Dad."

Pop wagged a finger at him. "You left because you wanted to. You've always hated this town and I don't know why. Now you want me to leave here. Ever since your mother died. That's been your plan, your scheme."

Michael shook his head. "All right, Dad. Calm down."

"I *am* calm."

"Forget about it." Michael walked out of the room and headed for the stairs.

"Forget about it?" Pop called after him. "Is that a joke? Do you really think I will?"

———————◆———————

Michael went back to the dining room. He felt upset that their conversation had gone so wrong. Now he wondered if his family had heard it all. The three were in the kitchen, washing up the dishes.

Colleen was putting the stew into a plastic container. She looked at him sympathetically.

"I'm going to take a walk," Michael said. He walked to the front door, nearly bumping into his father along the way.

Pop said lightly, "Let's play checkers. We haven't played in a long time."

"I don't want to play checkers. You cheat," he said.

Pop sounded affronted. "How can I cheat at checkers?"

"You always find a way," Michael said. He wondered where he'd put his coat. "And you tip the board over when you know you've lost."

"Get the board, son," Pop said.

Michael realized that his coat was still in the car. "I'm taking a walk. Ask Ethan to play."

Pop came close and said quietly, "You don't like me very much, do you?"

Michael's hand was on the doorknob. He gazed at his father without answering.

"That's okay, you know," Pop said. "You can love someone but not like them sometimes."

"That's a good thing, Dad," Michael said.

After retrieving his coat from the car, Michael walked down Braddock Street, past the wood and stone houses, the neatly trimmed uniform-sized lawns, the mature trees with their bare branches, and the memories of people long gone who once called to him from their porches.

He walked past the Sizemore house, now looking run-down and faded. But, in a flash, he saw it as it once was—bright and new. And there was Kathy Sizemore in the driveway, waving to him, her smile as radiant as he remembered, her hair a golden glow, and her slender body made all the more attractive by a baggy university sweatshirt and tight jeans. She was his first love. His heart pounded hard as it once had when he saw her. Then she climbed into her white 1966 Mustang and drove away, smiling again as she passed.

How can the past look so real? he thought. He knew that Kathy was alive and well and living in Nevada. He'd read it on one of those social networks. *So, how can she be here now, looking exactly as she did then?*

A man Michael didn't know stepped out of the front door. Giving Michael a wary look, the man went to the empty, cracked driveway and stooped down to pick up a newspaper.

For a fleeting moment, Michael felt a familiar longing—the kind that only a visit to Hope Springs seemed to stir in him. He wouldn't trade his years with Colleen for anyone or anything in the world. But he still longed for the innocence of that first love, the early excitement of youth. The tingle he got in his gut when he first held Kathy's hand. The warm grip that pressed his heart when they kissed. The ease of their conversations, the pleasure of their outings, the single-mindedness and naivete of their companionship.

He remembered one picnic with Kathy that should have been a true disaster. The sodas were warm, the sandwiches dry, and the dessert she'd made special for the occasion got crushed under a sneaker that fell off the back shelf of his car when he stopped too fast at a light. But they were undaunted. Little disasters turned into little jokes. Michael laughed harder that day than he'd ever laughed before or since. Even when it rained and they had to dash into the shelter of the gazebo in the park, they laughed. As the rain drummed like fingers on the roof, he turned to her as if in slow motion, her hair fanning wet and her smile so wide that the dimples showed on both sides of her mouth. Her eyes were half open, blinking away the drops that fell from her forehead. She was so beautiful, almost transcendent, he thought. Then she said, laughing, "What a perfect day," and they exchanged a look of such purity and joy that Michael knew something had changed in his perception of the world. The feelings were so strong that he prayed to God to freeze the moment. He wanted to hold onto every sensation, every impression, as if he'd come alive for the first time in his life—as if in one moment, all the best moments of life could be contained.

He wondered then if there might be other moments in his life that stood like this one: fixed in time, but somehow outside of it. Maybe such moments were glimpses of something like Heaven.

But that moment with Kathy had passed and Michael was later left with an indescribable ache, a longing, which he coveted and regretted at the same time. Summer ended. Michael and Kathy went their separate ways, to different colleges, and onto whatever the future held for them. But the mysterious longing continued for Michael. He felt hints of it when he married Colleen and when his children were born. There were moments, but never quite *the* moment he yearned to recapture. So he adjusted his expectations and tried to bury his longing.

Having been away from Hope Springs for most of his life, he had to wonder why the town brought back his memories more vividly than anywhere else on earth.

It troubled him. At times, it felt as if the town was taunting him. What was the point of longing for what he couldn't have? *Leave me alone*, he wanted to shout. *Can't you see that I have the problem of my father to solve? I need to find a job!*

Downtown Hope Springs had changed more than he'd realized during the drive into town. Spaces that had been empty, covered with notices and bills, were now inhabited by small boutique-type shops. Hayes Department Store, the headquarters of good taste and fashion for so many years, was now filled with condos. The Coliseum—for years the place to go for movies before it closed—was now reopened as an art house cinema. The marquee announced a movie he'd never heard of.

Mr. Pierce, the owner of Michelle's Ice Cream Parlor, stood with his broom in hand under the long pink awning that stretched out to the curb. He waved and Michael waved back, even though he was certain Mr. Pierce didn't know who he was. Michael then remembered that Michelle's was originally opened as a "gay nineties" ice cream parlor back in the day. At a glance, he now saw that it had a 1950s diner décor.

Michael passed by a tattoo parlor called "Tattoos While-U-Wait." This gave Michael a momentary pause as he wondered if there was any other way to get a tattoo. *Mail order? Get one virtually online?*

Michael stopped into the Sunshine Florist shop and decided to take flowers to his mother's grave. He hadn't been there in a couple of years. A woman Michael vaguely remembered—from the Binnocek family, he thought—helped him pick out a colorful bouquet of carnations and daffodils with a sprinkling of angel's breath. He had no idea what was appropriate for a grave but tried to pick flowers he thought his mother would like.

With the basket in hand, Michael walked through town to St. Clare's Catholic Church, then behind it for another block to the graveyard. It was surrounded by a tall wrought iron fence with a *fleur-de-lis* pattern serving as spears on the top of each pike. He went to the pedestrian entrance, next to the large double-doored gate, and went in.

As a boy, he'd been fascinated by the graveyard. The older sections contained gravestones going all the way back to the 1800s, when Hope Springs was established. He often wandered past the many markers, wondering about the people buried under them. Now, though, he strode directly to his mother's grave, nestled as it was next to a grove of strategically placed trees. He looked down at the angled bronze markers—one for Linda Marie Reynolds, with her final particulars, and the other for James Michael Reynolds, with his unfinished particulars.

He remembered once when the whole family had gone to the grave with his father. Ethan had asked Pop very innocently, "Is it strange standing here, looking down at your name on your future grave?"

Without missing a beat, Pop replied, "As long as I'm standing here looking down on the grave, it doesn't bother me at all."

Michael thought of his mother but never imagined her there in the graveyard. The ghost of her memory didn't belong with the dead.

He reverently placed the flowers on his mother's plot of earth. The ground was soft and mosslike. Since childhood, Michael always felt that cemetery earth was too squishy, as if you might suddenly sink into one of the graves below. The flowers looked artificially colorful against the brown grass, the bronze marker, and the gray stone. The sun disappeared behind thick clouds.

Lowering his head, Michael made the Sign of the Cross and began to pray for the soul of his mom. Then he began to pray for his dad ... but the words escaped him. What did he want to tell God? What did he want God to do? Fix his father, find him a job, make everything all right?

He exhaled slowly, a sigh coming from a very deep place. He thought about the saints he had studied—men and women who overcame great physical and emotional trauma to glorify God with their lives. But losing a job wasn't the kind of trauma that shaped a man like him into a saint. He couldn't think of a book about a saint who'd merely lost a job. Who cared about that? Growing old wasn't compelling reading either. Who would write a book about such a thing? Why would they? No one ever claimed a great victory for God because an unemployment form had been filled out correctly. Or proclaimed the wondrous works of the Lord because someone had grown old. How was God glorified in memory loss, temper tantrums, loss of bodily functions, and bedpans?

Michael stood up, surprised by a feeling of despair that caused him to shiver. No one had told him that losing your job was like losing a loved one. No one said that grief would feel like dry heaves. No one had warned him that he would feel so completely empty inside.

Michael left the graveyard and made his way downtown following one of the back streets. He remembered that there was a nursing home housed in what was once someone's mansion—a monstrous red-stone building that looked like a set from a horror movie and had spooked him when he was a boy. It wouldn't take him too far out of the way to stop in and get information, he figured. He tried to think of what it was called. Something soothing, about a garden, he thought.

He walked a little further and suddenly he realized he was in front of it. A huge structure that had clearly been expanded since he'd last noticed it.

The Faded Flower Retirement Home, the sign said.

"The Faded Flower?" Michael said, amused. "What an unfortunate name."

CHAPTER 3

E THAN SAT in the big easy chair in the living room, headphones clamped to his head. His favorite music—a playlist he'd organized before the trip—thumped away in his ears. He gazed at the room and wished he'd brought his laptop computer. He'd left it behind as a concession to his mother. Now he regretted the concession as he sat by himself, the family scattered for different reasons. There wasn't really anything for him to do. He thought about turning on the television but didn't know which one actually worked.

He slid the headphones off for a moment and listened. In a distant part of the basement, Pop was banging around the old coal furnace. It was supposed to be cold that night and Pop said he wanted the furnace stoked properly. Ethan could hear Pop through the vent in the wall, though he didn't know exactly what his grandfather was doing. He recognized the sound of the squeaky iron door opening; maybe Pop was shoveling the coal in, or opening and closing flues. He'd grown up with those sounds when he had visited, and they often greeted him early on a cold winter's morning or at night as they were going to sleep. His father had wanted Pop to get a new and more efficient furnace, but Pop wasn't interested. The coal furnace was like an old friend, Pop had said at the time.

Ethan wondered where Pop found coal to burn.

He put his headphones back on. The music seemed to serve as a soundtrack to his thoughts.

Ch-ch-ch-ch-changes, David Bowie sang. Ethan was a fan of music from the 1970s and 80s. To hear Bowie sing about changes seemed ironic, since Ethan now sat in a room that defied change. The magazines on the end table could have been pulled from a time capsule from 1968. There was an old *Guideposts* with Johnny Unitas in uniform on the cover. Billy Graham's *Decision* magazine had a story about a British pop star named Cliff Richard. *Stories from the Wild West* chronicled the career of Wild Bill Hickock. And beneath these were a handful of women's magazines that defied the imagination: *True Confessions*, in which sordid tales of love were told anonymously. Had his grandmother actually read this junk?

Ethan sunk deeper into the chair. He found comfort in this room, even in the whole house. It was like a speedbump to the fast-moving changes that marked his world—new technologies, new social rules, new conflicts, new *everything*. Where he had once noticed change only in seasons, or moves from one class to another, or one grade to another, or the year his voice broke, now the changes came from every direction. He was going to *college* now. He had to make decisions about his future. He had to roll *with the changes*—to quote REO Speedwagon.

That's why it was reassuring to come to his grandfather's. Change wasn't an issue here. At least it wasn't until now.

Ethan felt a tight fist of anxiety push into his stomach. If Pop had to go into a nursing home, then they'd sell this house and another thread to the past would be cut. If his dad didn't find a new job, then they might have to sell their house and move to a different part of the country. It shouldn't matter if Ethan went to college or if he didn't.

Ethan's mind spun with the contradictions of his feelings. Hadn't he lectured his father about the error of staying in the same job, doing mind-numbing variations of the same thing, for such a long time? This change was good for his dad. It seemed wrong, somehow, for a man to become so entrenched into a single way of life. Where was the adventure? Where was the spark? But Ethan also felt hypocritical by demanding change from his father but resisting this change for Pop. Weren't both necessary?

Ethan tried to shrug off the questions. He didn't have any answers, nor did he expect to come up with any. Things simply happened and you had to roll along with them. Was it really that easy? Wasn't God watching over them—maybe even orchestrating the changes? Or was he watching from the bench, a nonplayer, a mere spectator? Ethan sometimes wondered.

Taking out his phone, Ethan checked one app and then another, noting what his friends were posting and talking about. He wanted to put his thoughts to them, to see what they'd say. There were already a few messages for him, asking how it was going there "at the back of beyond."

That was another irony about his world of change. The technology had expanded and taken over everyone's lives. It became ever-present and eternal. The internet would always be there. Whether or not Ethan moved to another house, city, or country—he could still log on and chat with people as if they were in the same room. Yet, he and his friends also admitted to feeling degrees of loneliness they'd never known before. Text on a screen couldn't replace flesh and blood.

"Ahem," Pop cleared his throat. He was standing next to the couch with an old checkerboard spread like a tray in his hands. "You must be trying to solve the problems of the world."

Taking off his headphones, Ethan looked up at his grandfather. He still hadn't forgotten about Pop's outburst earlier and the uncharacteristic way he'd lashed out at them. Colleen had privately assured Ethan and Madison that it wasn't really Pop; it was his illness that was acting then. But Ethan still worried about something like that happening again—and how he would handle it.

Pop held out the checkerboard. "Let's play."

"Only if you promise not to cheat," Ethan said as playfully as he could.

Pop feigned an indignant look. "Don't *you* start."

Ethan found a rickety old TV dinner stand in the corner of the room and pulled it over, along with a folding metal chair that was stashed behind one of the televisions. Pop sat down in his favorite easy chair. They set up the pieces and started to play.

He gazed at Pop for a moment. His grandfather's remaining hair was whiter and thinner, the wrinkles deeper. There were broken red veins on his cheeks. Under his nose, a section of facial hair he'd missed with the razor. The game began, with moves and jumps.

Ethan thought about bringing up his decision about leaving college. Pop might understand. Or maybe he wouldn't. Wasn't his generation the one that valued a college education above everything else?

Pop abruptly tapped the table. The pieces rattled. "Are you going to just sit there and daydream? It's your move."

Ethan looked at the board. "Oh, yeah." He quickly moved a piece.

Pop jumped the piece Ethan had just moved, landing him at the end of the board. Pop clapped his hands. "Crown me."

Ethan stared at the board, unsure of how Pop's piece had wound up where it was.

"Your dad and I used to play all the time," Pop said while Ethan crowned the piece. "He was a very serious player. He acted like he was playing chess. That's no way to play checkers. Checkers is for fun. Chess is for brain cramps. I hope his walk helps him unwind a little."

"Me, too." But Ethan didn't believe it would. He suspected the walk would make his father all the more determined. To *solve the problems* of life. Make decisions about Pop and the house and a nursing home. Solve the crisis about a job.

Pop nodded as if he knew what Ethan was thinking. "He's got a lot on his mind. He's on edge. It's the way of the world—a man works for all those years and what happens? He's let go. The same happened to me when I worked at the coal mine. No sooner had I gotten out of the mine and into a supervisor's position than they shut down the whole operation."

"What did you do?"

"I went to work for the railroad." Pop chuckled. "Now *that* was a growth industry. I sure knew how to pick 'em."

Ethan remembered his grandfather coming home from his shift at the Hope Springs railway station wearing his chipped black work boots and dark blue uniform. For years Ethan believed Pop was actually an engineer on a train, wearing a red scarf around his neck and tooting the whistle. Only as an adult did Ethan learn that

Pop was actually in charge of local freight and never actually rode on the trains.

"Your father needs to have a little more faith," Pop said. "The Lord will provide. He always has. It's the only way I've made it. You live this long and you see some bad times. But, even at its worst, God was there. We never went hungry. We always had a roof over our heads. God has been good." He pointed a bony finger at Ethan. "Don't you forget it."

"I'll try not to." Ethan double jumped Pop's pieces and landed in a crown square on Pop's side of the board.

Pop looked appalled. "What was that? What do you call that move?"

Ethan shrugged. "It was a move. I got your pieces and now I'm waiting to be crowned."

"You can't move like that in checkers."

"Sure, I can. It was a double jump and I got your pieces."

Pop shook his head.

"Pop, you promised," Ethan said. He knew this was how it would be. This was part of Pop's strategy. It was as much a part of the game as anything to do with checkers.

"Don't talk to me about promises. In all my years of checkers …" Pop scratched at his chin and then pointed at the board. "And I just had the one crowned! Jump a man when he gets crowned. That's not very Christian."

"It's in the rules," Ethan said.

"What rules?"

Ethan pulled out his phone. "I'll show you."

"Not on that contraption, you won't. I don't believe anything that spider's web has to say."

"But—"

"Put it back," Pop said firmly.

Ethan didn't move, wondering how far he could push Pop. They stared at each other.

"*Put. It.—* "

Ethan put the crowned piece back onto the board.

Pop smiled. "Good boy."

Ethan grumbled, "I see what you're doing."

"Quit talking and move."

"I'm afraid to."

"Go on. Don't be a sissy."

Ethan carefully moved his piece. "Nothing wrong with *that* move, I hope."

Pop scrutinized the board. "Nope."

While Pop decided his next move, Ethan leaned back. This seemed like as good a time as any to broach the subject. "Pop, I've got a problem."

"What's her name?"

"It's not a *her*."

"It isn't? Then you *do* have a problem." Pop chuckled.

Ethan leaned forward again. He tugged at a thread that had come loose from the end of his sleeve. "I don't want to go back to college."

"You don't?" Pop looked surprised. "But we talked about that. You have to go to college to meet the coeds!"

"I'll meet them some other time," Ethan replied. "Later, maybe. Besides, that's no reason to go to college."

"It's more fun than getting an education."

Ethan gazed at his grandfather. "You're not helping me."

Pop nodded. "All right."

"I don't want to go, but Dad keeps saying I should."

"I thought you wanted a degree. Didn't you say it was the only way to get ahead in this world—what with all the techno-gadgets and thingamajigs you use?"

"I never said that. *Dad* says that."

"I see," Pop said thoughtfully. "So, have you told your father?"

"I've mentioned it, but he won't listen." Ethan hesitated. "He doesn't think I have a plan. I have a plan. I just don't have his ambition."

"What's your plan?"

Ethan moved a game piece. "I'm going to hang around, experience life, and try to figure things out."

"Sounds expensive," Pop said. "And it's not much of a plan, as plans go."

Ethan fought to keep his defensiveness at bay. "It's not a plan the way you or Dad think of plans. But that's the difference between our generations. We don't think the way you do." Ethan paused.

"What way is that?"

"Conventionally. No offense."

Pop smiled. "None taken."

"I've seen where office jobs lead. There's a better way of doing it."

"Like what?" asked Pop.

"That's what I need to figure out."

Pop didn't say anything for a moment, then he gave his shoulders a slight lift. "I'm the wrong person to ask right now. There are certain people who think I'm not of a sound mind. But maybe you're right. Maybe my generation has it all wrong. You live and you work and you raise a family, and it all ends with ... with what?"

"That's what I want to know," Ethan said.

"The future is what you make of it, Ethan. If going to college will give you the tools to make it something good and worthwhile, then go to college. If it won't, then skip it. You're a smart kid. You'll do the right thing."

"Thanks, Pop."

They resumed the game and Ethan wondered if that was it—if that was as much as could be said on the subject.

Pop moved his piece. "You get used to it, you know."

"Used to what?"

"The idea of death."

Ethan was perplexed. Had they been talking about death?

Pop slowly touched one of the pieces. "You get to this age and you have to make peace with it. Make peace or go crazy. And you learn not to make any long-term plans."

Ethan decided to roll with the conversation. "Like what?" he asked.

"Don't buy green bananas anymore."

Ethan laughed.

"You never know if you'll be around by the time they ripen," Pop said. "No magazine subscriptions that last more than a year. Don't pay extra for warranties on appliances."

Ethan made a move. Then, with a look of pure delight, Pop grabbed a piece and heartily double jumped his way toward Ethan's end of the board. "Ha! Take that! Double jump!" He smiled with self-satisfaction as he claimed his victims. "And you thought you could take advantage of an old man. I know your ruse, using that conversation about college to distract me."

"But, Pop—"

"It's no good trying to haggle your way out of it."

"Pop—"

"Forget it, Ethan. The victory is mine."

"But you just double jumped your own pieces."

Pop looked down at the board, his face frozen in a half-smile, his brow knitted above the center of his nose. "Well. Yes. I did that on purpose," he said. "It was . . . to protect my pieces. You can take them off of the board and save them for when you really need them."

Ethan folded his arms. "I've never heard of that."

"It's the way I've always played. Eighty years. *Always.*"

Ethan was unconvinced. "You taught me how to play and I've never heard of that rule. Put those pieces back."

"It's . . ." Pop paused. Ethan could almost hear the wheels turning in Pop's mind. "It's an upper-level rule."

"It is not. Put them back."

"It's for expert players."

"Pop—"

It was another showdown. Ethan held his gaze. Pop snorted and put his pieces back onto the board. Scowling, he said, "I thought you were ready for the pro games but apparently you're not. You want to be an amateur all your life."

"That's right," Ethan said.

"Not another word. Just move!" Pop growled.

Unsure whether Pop was serious or not, Ethan moved a piece.

"Don't be silly," Pop said softly.

Ethan looked over at Pop. "What do you mean?"

Pop scrutinized the checkerboard, his cheeks suddenly going crimson. "Now, wait a minute. Let me think."

"Think about what?"

Pop stared at the board longer, then sat back abruptly and said, "I don't want to play anymore."

"What?" Ethan asked. Had he hurt Pop's feelings? "Forget it. Put your pieces back on the board if it means that much to you."

Pop shook his head. "It's not that."

"Then what's wrong?" asked Ethan.

Pop looked at Ethan with a pained expression on his face. "Am I black or red?"

Pop settled down in front of the television while Ethan packed up the checkerboard and checkers and put away the small table. Then the front door burst open and Colleen and Madison walked in with packages and a large cake box. A blast of cold air chased them in.

Ethan noticed that his mother was red-faced. "I didn't expect to take so long," she puffed. "What time is it?"

Pop looked at his watch. "Two—"

"Never mind. It must be after four at least." Colleen took the cake box out to the kitchen but called back, "We would've been home sooner but Thelma at the bakery had to tell me all the latest gossip."

"She talked about everybody who died," Madison added unhappily.

"She's a walking obituary column," Pop said. "Nobody kicks the bucket around here without telling her first."

Madison rolled her eyes. "She couldn't remember what kind of frosting we wanted."

"But she remembered down to the button what clothes everyone was buried in," Colleen said.

"Thelma's a couple of cookies short of a dozen, if you know what I mean," Pop said. "Too many years sniffing vanilla extract."

"Where's Michael?" Colleen asked.

"He said I should move out of the house, so I shot him," Pop said. "He's buried in the basement."

"Then I shouldn't have bought such a large cake," Colleen said. She went back to the kitchen. Cupboard doors began opening and closing. Final preparations for the evening birthday party were underway.

That was a classic Mom *move,* Ethan thought. Somehow—and Ethan didn't know how—she had the ability to take any potentially awkward or tense situation and diffuse it. She had done that Ethan's entire life. Battles with teachers, conflicts with neighbors, a falling out with a friend . . . his mother navigated those turbulent waters with ease and grace. His dad had once said that she was like a duck: on the surface she appeared calm, but beneath the surface her legs were paddling wildly.

He wondered how long she could keep the peace in this situation. He knew that his dad believed that the only way through some conflicts was with a face-to-face, knock-down-drag-out argument. Confront it, get it all out honestly and candidly, and then an answer would present itself. But his mother's smooth diversions, her uncanny instincts, might get in the way.

A few minutes later, Colleen reappeared from the kitchen and announced that it would be a good idea to go up to the attic and look for some costumes for the party.

"Costumes?" Pop asked.

"It's a costume party," Colleen explained. "Didn't Minnie tell you?"

"No," Pop said with a snort. "And she knows better than to think I'm going to dress up in a silly costume."

"I thought you loved costume parties," Madison said. "Don't you remember the Fourth of July, the one before Grandma died? You dressed up as Paul Revere."

"If I did, it was for her. Now I'd look like a fool."

Colleen was undeterred. "Come on. It'll be fun. I'm sure the attic is full of great things."

"Any clothes up there were digested by moths years ago," Pop said.

Colleen went to him and tugged at his arm. "No birthday presents for you if you don't make the effort."

Groaning, Pop pulled himself to his feet. "All right, but everyone else is coming up, too. I won't face the monsters alone."

The four of them ascended the stairs to the attic. The floorboards creaked loudly as they entered. Colleen kept pushing at the rippling edges of the yellowing wallpaper, as if her magic touch would restore the ancient glue. Ethan's suitcase sat on one of the four single beds that lined the wall. He fondly remembered that this room had been the setting for a lot of kids' play between the cousins, especially after the adults had told them *for the last time* to go to sleep.

"Oh!" Colleen exclaimed. She wrinkled her nose and opened the two dormer windows to let in some fresh air. "It smells terribly musty."

"I don't come up here much," Pop said.

Two old wardrobes sat on opposite sides of a doorway into the unfinished section of the attic. Colleen and Madison attacked the wardrobes. Pop opened the door that led to the space under the eaves. He reached in and yanked the chain to a single bulb that hung just inside.

Ethan followed him in. That door—and all the junk that had collected behind it—had always been a source of fascination for Ethan as he was growing up. There was an old pedal-powered sewing machine, some broken chairs, and the shell of a console record player (Pop had probably sold its innards). A box of records—78s and 45s—had tipped over, the black vinyl looking like pools of oil on the floor. Ethan knelt down and glanced at the artists. Some he'd heard of; some he hadn't. Tommy Dorsey, Jimmy Dorsey, Bing Crosby, the Mills Brothers, and Glenn Miller he knew. Pat Boone, Eddie Fisher, Woody Herman, and Artie Shaw weren't familiar. The labels were a variety of silver, burgundy, white, and black.

Old toys that had been given to his dad and his uncle Dennis for their birthdays or Christmases long gone also gathered there. The remains of a large plastic pinball game leaned against the wall, one of its three legs missing. A child's version of an adult workbench rested among thick cobwebs. Ethan knew it was his father's—even now the various wooden tools were still in their proper places. A couple of early versions of handheld game devices lay with cracked screens; one was a football game; the other was something called Merlin. There were board games, a toy dashboard with steering wheel, a cassette player, and model cars. Railroad tracks littered the floor while the train cars themselves lay like corpses nearby. Ethan remembered that the running of the trains around the Christmas tree was a beloved family tradition. Pop would spend hours setting it up, and then with great fanfare one lucky grandchild would throw the power switch. That was the second thing that announced the arrival of Christmas. The first, of course, was the arrival of the Sears Christmas Wish Book.

There was a small battery-operated shooting gallery with cardboard ducks that quacked their way from one end to the other. The goal was to hit as many as you could with the little plastic balls that shot from a toy rifle. Legend had it that Uncle Dennis often shot Michael—and once got him solidly in the eye with one.

Old trunks sat like small boats in the sea of debris. Pop moved from one to another, throwing open the lids to check the contents. "Let's try this one," he said, then motioned to Ethan to help him carry it out.

Colleen and Madison descended upon the trunk, jabbering as they pulled the clothes out. Madison marveled over her grandmother's wedding dress, now a pale yellow with dirty stitching. Colleen looked at Pop's railroad uniform and a few token citations and medals from his days in the military reserves. Ethan admired a dark suit made of a burnt orange corduroy with wide lapels and bell-bottomed trouser legs.

They pressed the clothes to themselves or made Ethan serve as a model. He didn't mind putting on an old uniform or shirt, but he drew the line at a girdle or bra.

Pop looked on with a childlike expression on his face. "I'd forgotten about most of this stuff. Look at this." He grabbed an old fedora and dropped it on his head. "What a classic. Humphrey Bogart, huh?"

"More like Jerry Lewis on a bad day," Ethan said.

Colleen pulled out a tall trophy with a silver dart on the top. "You should have this out on display."

"Good idea," Michael said from the staircase. "People can impale themselves on it as they walk past it."

"Oh, Michael, just in time. We're looking for costumes for the party," Colleen said.

Michael gave her a weak smile and moved into the room. Ethan knew his father's expressions well enough to recognize that the walk hadn't helped anything.

Pop held the dart trophy and gazed at it fondly. "The Interfaith Dart League—1963. We beat the Brownfield Synagogue in the playoffs. I guess that showed 'em who *really* knows God."

"That's not funny," Madison said.

"Here's a school certificate," Colleen announced, holding up a broken frame. "You got it for perfect attendance in fourth grade."

"Mrs. Skillman. What a wonderful teacher she was." Pop paused for a moment. "It broke her heart when she had to stop teaching."

Michael flipped through a small black book. "I want to know who Judith McKenzie was. You have two stars next to her name."

"What is that?"

"An address book."

Pop grabbed for it. "Give me that."

Michael held the book away. "Not until you tell me who these people are."

"People I knew before I got married. Most of them are dead now."

"Did you put the stars in before or after they died?" Madison asked.

Colleen gasped. "Madison!"

Madison gave her an impish smile.

"It's a date book," Michael explained to her as he thumbed through the pages. "You have three stars next to someone named Anastasia. And Kathy Fitzgibbons got *four* stars."

"Pop, please don't tell me you were *rating* those girls," Madison said.

Pop hung his head in an insincere show of shame.

"Men are disgusting!" Madison snorted.

"You think women are any different?" Pop asked. He leaned to Ethan and said in a conspiratorial tone, "Kathy was a knockout back then."

"What about now?"

Pop shook his head and said, "I saw her at the grocery store the other day. She's had so many face lifts that she could use her Adam's apple as a nose."

Colleen put her hands up in protest. "Stop, Pop."

"She coughed and nearly knocked her fake eyelashes off."

"I see you've got *five* stars next to Linda Mardell," Michael said.

"Who was that?" asked Ethan.

"Your grandmother."

Ethan blushed. "Oh." He had forgotten her maiden name.

Colleen held up a piece of paper with flowery writing. "Here's your wedding certificate. There's a photo taped to it, too."

Ethan and Madison gathered around to look. The photo was black-and-white, cracked around the edges. Pop stood on the steps of a church, a tall and striking young man in a dark suit, his hands at his side. Grandma stood next to him wearing the dress they'd just found, and a bridal veil. They looked uncomfortable, as if having their picture taken was the worst part of the day.

They handed the photo to Pop, who looked at it for a long time. He made a noise that sounded like a cough, then stood up. "I'm going to put on some coffee."

Colleen waved a hand to stop him. "I'll do it."

He shooed her away. "I know how, thanks."

They listened to Pop shuffle down the stairs to the second floor, then onward to the staircase leading to the main floor.

"Maybe this wasn't such a good idea," Colleen said.

"We can't baby him," Michael said. He pulled some folded papers from his back pocket. "At least that's what the manager said at the Faded Flower."

"The Faded Flower?" Colleen asked.

"A retirement home right here in town," Michael said. "I don't know why I didn't think about it before. It's been there for years."

"I don't think this is a good time to talk about it," Colleen said.

Michael gazed at her. "There will never be a good time to talk about it."

Ethan picked up an old leather-backed book. It was a Challoner-Rheims version of the New Testament. He flipped open the cover and read the distinctive pen-and-ink cursive: "For James, from Mother and Father—1949." The pages were pulling away from the seam, and some of the verses had been lightly underlined with a pencil.

"We haven't had any serious problems since we arrived," Colleen said.

"He still cheats at checkers," Ethan said. He thought his mother was trying to sound hopeful and positive.

"That's not Alzheimer's," Colleen said.

Ethan idly flipped through the Bible. A bookmark took him to the Gospel of St. John, where chapter 3, verse 16 leapt out at him: "For God so loved the world that He gave His only-begotten Son, that those who believe in Him may not perish, but may have life everlasting. "

Michael shook his head. "What about his outburst this morning?"

"We all have outbursts," Colleen argued. "You've had a few yourself."

"You can say that again," Madison said under her breath. Ethan offered her a sympathetic look.

Michael shot a look at Madison, then shoved the flyer back into his pocket.

From elsewhere in the house, Ethan could hear the sound of the pipes rumbling—then silence. Pop must have given them a good kick.

"I'm only saying that it may be too soon to talk about retirement homes and moving him from this house," Colleen said.

Michael frowned. "Minnie knows more about it than we do. You heard her on the porch. She said he needs someone to watch over him. The Faded Flower has areas with all levels of care."

Colleen sighed. "We have to choose the right time to talk to him."

"I don't know how long we can wait. The manager at the Faded Flower said we must get the tests done for a proper diagnosis. A doctor's educated guesswork isn't enough."

"How will we talk him into that?" Madison asked.

Michael shook his head. "God only knows."

They carried potential costumes and other memorabilia down to the living room. Pop greeted them as he came in from the kitchen. He noticed the book in Ethan's hand.

"My old Bible," he said.

"I was looking at some of the verses you marked," Ethan said.

"My parents marked them," Pop explained. "They made me memorize those verses."

"Do you still remember them?"

"Try me."

Ethan turned to one of the pages in the back. "James chapter 1, verses 2 and 3."

Pop closed his eyes and said, "My brethren, count it all joy when ye fall into divers temptations; knowing this, that the trying of your faith worketh patience." He opened his eyes and looked directly at Michael. "Not bad for a senile old man who can't take care of himself. And still has very good hearing." He gave Michael a toothy smile.

Michael tipped his head to Ethan. "Take a look at Titus 2." But before Ethan could find it, Michael recited: "Aged men be sober, grave, temperate, sound in faith, in charity, in patience."

"Yep, that's a good one," Pop said. "But I like Ephesians 6, where it says to 'obey your parents in the Lord, for this is right. Honor your father and mother that it may be well with you, and that you may live long on the earth.'"

"The rest of that is pretty good, too," Michael countered. "And fathers, do not provoke your children to anger."

"I also like—" Pop began, but he couldn't think of another verse. He grabbed the Bible from Ethan. "Give me that book."

"What're you going to do, hit someone with it?" Ethan asked. He was starting to feel anxious again. This game of dueling Bible verses had an awful edge to it.

Colleen interceded. "I think that's enough for now. Minnie will be here soon. No bloodshed before the party."

Pop pouted in a way that caused Ethan to think it was a joke. "No respect. No respect at all." Pop spun toward the kitchen angrily, and Ethan was alarmed to realize that he was serious.

"Dad, wait," Michael said.

Pop held up a hand. "No. I'm going to make some coffee."

"You're making *more* coffee?" Colleen asked.

"Why? Did you already make some?" Pop asked her.

Colleen looked confused. "No," she said. "*You* did."

"No, I didn't," Pop said.

"Then what did you just do in the kitchen?" Michael asked.

"When?"

"Just now."

"I wasn't in the kitchen. I've been standing here talking to you." He looked impatiently at Michael. "Quit joking around. You make me nervous."

"I'm not joking," Michael said.

"Stop it!" Pop shouted. "You're trying to make me think I need help. I don't! Do you hear me? I'm going to make coffee. For the *first* time." He stormed back to the kitchen.

Michael and Colleen looked at each other. Ethan chewed at his lower lip.

Madison gave them an amused look. "I hope everyone wants a lot of coffee."

CHAPTER 4

M ICHAEL WAS in no mood to dress up. For the sake of Colleen, he conceded to wear his father's Army jacket. It was the most he would do. His father had been baiting him all afternoon. Michael had tried to deflect the comments good-naturedly, but he could feel his patience wearing thin.

Colleen dressed up in an old flapper's dress she found in another trunk.

"Pretty racy, even for a Catholic," Michael observed.

"Your mother wasn't always a Catholic," Colleen reminded him. "She came from a family of Methodists who were downright worldly."

Michael wondered if the skirt was too short and the neckline too low. He didn't mind—but didn't want Pop's friends to have collective heart attacks.

Michael noticed that Ethan had made himself scarce until it was time for the party. He could sense his son's uneasiness. That last encounter with Pop about the coffee had clearly shaken the boy. No doubt Ethan would have hidden in the attic if Colleen hadn't summoned him out to help with preparations. She demanded that he dress up in one of Pop's old suits for the party: a double-breasted jacket and cuffed pants. It was too large. Ethan looked as if he might vanish inside of it.

Madison disappeared for a while. When Michael saw her again, she was wearing fake stick-on tattoos on her arms, purchased from the shop around the corner. She had decided to dress as a biker—though she wore her own T-shirt and torn jeans, looking pretty much as she always did. Every now and then she'd jingle some car keys and mention her Harley that she'd parked in the back. Later she found a small square box to roll up in one of her T-shirt sleeves. "It's supposed to be a box of cigarettes," she explained to her dad.

Michael kept an eye on Pop. What was really going on inside his father's mind? How aware was Pop of his condition? Was he pretending not to see the changes in himself, or were they genuinely invisible to him? Michael remembered something a comedian had once said: "Hey, the good thing about Alzheimer's is that you're always meeting new people." The line was funny then. It wasn't as funny now.

At some point before the party started, Michael heard Madison say to Ethan, "It's all so *depressing*. I feel like this is going to be the last thing we ever do in this house. And it's not going to be fun at all."

Michael felt discouraged. This party was not going to play out the way Colleen had hoped. Somehow, he knew it as a certainty. The stage was set; it was unavoidable now. It was going to end in tears. The question was, whose tears?

Ultimately, Pop didn't dress up. Not much. He wore the hat he had pulled from the trunk. He announced it was more than enough costume for his birthday.

The big surprise was Aunt Minnie. She made a grand entrance dressed in a large bunny rabbit costume. Michael was dumbfounded. He couldn't imagine what made her think it was a good idea. Her ears flapped from her hooded head like deflated balloons. The bodysuit sagged in all the wrong places. Her cottontail made her look incontinent.

"Somebody, hide me," she gasped. "Old Man Hennessy is after me."

"Why? Is it rabbit season?" Pop asked.

She puffed, "It's *Minnie* season. He's been trying to get me to marry him. When he saw this outfit, he went wild."

"I keep telling Hennessy to stop reading those old magazines," Pop said. "They're bad for his heart."

Someone on the porch coughed and Aunt Minnie turned. "Good heavens, I almost forgot."

She moved aside so a young man could enter. Michael guessed he was in his early thirties, maybe older. He was tall and lanky, with limp black hair that lay in sharp contrast to his pasty white skin. Large round black-framed glasses were perched precariously on his nose. He wore a white lab coat. Michael thought he looked like a doctor from a bad high school drama production.

"Elmer Fudd?" Pop said.

"Elliot, actually," the man replied. "Elmer is my brother."

Aunt Minnie quickly explained the labyrinth of family associations on her side of the family that had resulted in Elliot's existence, concluding with: "So he's your cousin, second or third removed."

"Removed from what?" Michael asked. "Is that your costume, or are you really a doctor?"

"I'm a doctor, of sorts."

"Aha!" Pop cried out, spinning to Michael. "A doctor! So, you've called for reinforcements. Well, I won't go. You'll have to drag me kicking and screaming out of here. The neighbors will talk. There'll be pictures in the paper and on the interweb." Pop grabbed Elliot's hand and made a fuss over checking up his sleeves. "Where are they?"

"Where are what?" poor Elliot asked, looking at Aunt Minnie helplessly.

"The secret hypodermics. The hidden sedatives."

"Cut it out, Dad," Michael said.

"I don't trust you," Pop said while making a show of frisking Elliot. "One minute I'll be drinking some punch, and the next minute I'll be in a round rubber room eating a box of crayons."

"I wish I'd known you like crayons," Aunt Minnie said. "I would've gotten you some for your birthday."

Elliot looked bewildered. "This is an interesting branch of the family."

"I could use some help in the kitchen," Colleen said. Michael recognized her attempt to disarm the moment.

The birthday guests began to show up. Most were Pop's age or older.

Michael asked Ethan to play doorman and help some of them to the various chairs they'd set up around the room. The women smelled of perfume and lotions; the men smelled of aftershave and old laundry. The air soon had a particular kind of scent. *Old age* was the only way Michael could describe it. Some of the guests dressed up in costumes that resembled the clothes they probably wore most days anyway. A lot of browns and blues, with some that were stained an undefinable color and some that were stained another.

One old fellow accented his appearance with an eye patch to look like a pirate. Others wore hats to look like various people who wore hats. One woman made an attempt to come as Scarlett O'Hara from *Gone with the Wind*, except that her bell-shaped dress was flat on one side and her hair was completely white. A few of the guests shook Ethan's hand and called him Michael.

Pop told anyone who asked that he was there as Humphrey Bogart. "You look more like Hubert Humphrey," one old man said.

Madison was put into service as a drinks girl and drifted through the crowd with a tray of white cups filled with punch or soft drinks. At one point, her T-shirt sleeve unrolled and the box fell into the lap of a woman who'd fallen asleep. She screamed and swatted the box away—scattering the cups on a nearby table like pins at a bowling alley. Only then did Michael realize that the box was a deck of playing cards.

At that moment Michael noticed how adult Madison seemed. Not so much because of her outfit, but because of the poise she had as she chatted with the older folks. She showed none of the self-consciousness Michael had seen with many kids her age. He felt a twinge of something strange. It might have been pride. Or maybe it was a sense of loss, knowing that she was growing up, and quickly.

"Time for the cake!" Colleen announced and headed for the kitchen.

Pop sat in his usual chair, the seat of honor. Aunt Minnie sat nearby. Pop had his old address book in hand.

"I thought Linda told you to throw that out," Aunt Minnie was saying.

"Did she?"

"Good heavens, James, don't you remember? It was one of the worst fights you two ever had. Right after you got married. Linda didn't want you to keep it, and you wouldn't give it up."

Pop chuckled. "She had a jealous streak in her."

"She came to my house, crying her eyes out. She said she was never going back to you. She didn't want to be married to a playboy." Aunt Minnie laughed lightly. "Imagine her thinking of *you* as a playboy."

"It's not so far-fetched," Pop protested. "Not that anyone could compete with her in my heart, mind you," Pop said.

Michael thought Pop might regale everyone with the story of how he and his mother had met. Instead, he sat back in his chair and grabbed a handful of pretzels from a bowl. He watched everyone happily, proudly. "I wish she could be here now," he said, but Aunt Minnie had already turned away to talk to someone else.

They'd been married for over forty years, Michael thought. *How did he cope with the loss?* Michael could only remember the work to organize her funeral. He had hung around for a week after, just in case Pop needed anything. He didn't. At the time, Pop seemed strong, even stoic. If he wept, he wept in private. He spent most of his energy on all the other grief-stricken family members and friends.

Michael now looked around the room for some sign of his mother. It was as if Pop's clutter had driven her out, like weeds chasing the flowers from a garden. Sometimes Michael had flashes of boyhood memories—the quick moments with her. The pocket money to buy himself some sweets from the local candy shop. Her tender care after he'd been stung by a wasp. Her words of encouragement when Dicky Kane had bullied him at school. He saw her hunched over a table, playing gin rummy with whoever else wanted to play. He saw her milky white skin and small eyes, fragile fingers carefully arranging her hand of cards, or the delicate way she held a pen. She drew pictures for the kids. With a few strokes, she created whole scenes for their amusement: boats on the ocean, a kite in the sky, an odd-looking bear in a forest. More than any other memory, Michael saw her standing in the kitchen, her old slippers flapping against the worn linoleum as she moved between the stove and the sink—making her special pancakes for breakfast, or baking bread, or frying bacon with loud cracks and sizzles.

Michael looked at his father now and wondered what memories Pop had stored away. Or were they all slipping away?

Pop sat in his chair, gazing at the small gathering of family and friends. He wore a fixed smile but looked lost, Michael thought. And now the gaze went beyond them to the room, scanning the walls, and up to the ceiling. Was he thinking about moving out of the house? Then, as if to answer, Pop closed his eyes and shook his head.

What a terrible time, Michael thought. Gradual change was one thing, but this was like an assault. A lost job, a lost father ... both out of his control.

In a glow of yellow candlelight, Colleen stood in the doorway to the dining room. "Ta-da!" she exclaimed. There was scattered applause as she set the cake on the dining room table. "I couldn't get all eighty candles on, but I managed twenty-two. You can divide the number, or multiply it, or whatever."

"My wife the mathematician," Michael quipped.

One older woman hobbled to the table. "I can't eat any of that!" she said. "I'll go into a diabetic coma just *thinking* about it."

"Go on, James. Blow out your candles," a growly old fellow called from the back.

"We have to sing first," Colleen said. She led them in the "Happy Birthday" song.

For just a moment, Michael thought the evening might turn out all right after all.

Pop leaned forward toward the candles.

"Blow them all out in one try—if you can," someone challenged him.

"Ha." Pop leaned forward and then eyed the top of the cake. "What's this say? 'On Your Bar Mitzvah.' "

Colleen smiled and shrugged. "Thelma at the bakery dropped your birthday cake, so we had to come up with a quick alternative."

"After all these years, you're finally a man," Ethan said to Pop.

"Blow out the candles, Pop," Madison said. "The wax is dripping all over the cake."

"Make a wish," someone reminded him.

"Okay …" Pop took a deep breath and blew out the candles. Everyone applauded. "I didn't get my wish. I'm still old," he said.

"Now you can get a discount when you go bowling," another friend said.

"Great. They give me a discount when I don't have the energy to bowl." Pop laughed. Then he began to cough.

From where Michael stood, it looked as if Pop had sucked in some of the smoke from the candles.

As Pop continued to cough, Colleen stepped closer. "Pop, are you all right?"

Pop motioned at them, his coughing getting worse, becoming wheezier.

"Would you like some water?" Colleen asked.

He nodded sharply and she ran to the kitchen.

Pop coughed and gasped more loudly, his face turning bright red. Michael strode over and patted him on the back—softly at first, and then harder as Pop didn't seem to recover.

"Are you sure he's not having a heart attack?" a woman asked.

Pop tried to wave Michael away and leaned forward, his hands on the table, his hacking now wild and uncontrollable.

"Hurry with that water," Michael called out to the kitchen.

"I know how to do a tracheotomy!" the man with the pirate eye patch said. "Grab me a knife!"

From the kitchen came the sound of the pipes rumbling. Colleen cried out with pain. Michael was sure she had given the pipes a kick.

Pop's coughing and wheezing continued. His face turned red. He slid into a chair.

"Should we call 911?" Ethan asked.

"I'll call!" Madison said as she scrambled to pull her cell phone from one of her torn pockets.

"Do we need an ambulance?" Aunt Minnie asked. "Let him have some air. He just needs air."

"Ethan!" Michael called out. "Air!"

Ethan grabbed an old magazine and began to fan Pop.

Michael knelt down next to his father. "Try to breathe slowly." Pop looked at him wild-eyed.

"He can't breathe at all!" came another voice.

"Put your head between your legs," Scarlett O'Hara suggested.

Colleen limped across the room with a glass of water. Pop grabbed the glass and drank, water pouring down the sides of his mouth. Then he erupted with another cough, directly over the cake.

"Ew," the partygoers said.

Michael waved to Elliot. He'd been standing nearby, watching the scene unfold with a drink in hand and a breadstick hanging from his mouth. "Elliot, you're a doctor! Do something!"

Elliot looked shocked. "Actually—"

Aunt Minnie said, "Michael, he's not a—"

"*Just do something!*" Michael commanded. "CPR, mouth-to-mouth, anything!"

"But I'm a *veterinarian*," Elliot said.

Pop suddenly gasped, then wheezed, then slowly drew some air into his lungs, shallow at first, then long and deep, and held up his hands in surrender. Finding his voice, he rasped, "I'm fine! I'm fine!"

"Thank God," Elliot said and returned to his breadstick. "I haven't worked on people in years."

"And you're not starting with me," Pop growled, then said to Ethan, "You're going to give me pneumonia if you keep that up."

Ethan, lost in the excitement, had forgotten how frantically he'd been fanning the air. He now blushed and put the magazine down.

A nervous laugh of relief went through the small gathering.

"Well ...," Michael began, but Pop turned on him.

"What were *you* trying to accomplish?" Pop asked.

"What?"

"Beating me half to death. I didn't have anything lodged in my throat."

Michael looked at him, speechless.

Pop glared at the crowd. "And who told me to put my head between my legs?"

"What were we supposed to do? You were choking to death," Aunt Minnie said.

"I *wasn't* choking to death. It was all the smoke from that cake. I just breathed in wrong." Pop waved a hand at the slivers of smoke still rising from the candles.

"You turned bright red," Michael said.

"You overreacted. You *always* overreact," Pop said, his voice rising.

Oh no, Michael thought. *Here it comes.*

"A man coughs and you think he's dying. A man gets forgetful and you want to lock him away."

Michael flinched. "Why is it overreacting to worry about you? You were coughing. You looked like you were about to pass out. A man your age—"

"Ha! You see? A 'man my age.'" Pop pointed to the crowd. They collectively stepped back as if he held a gun. "You're witnesses. You heard it. A 'man my age'! What's my age have to do with coughing?"

"It could have been a real emergency," Aunt Minnie said.

"But it wasn't."

"But it could have been. At *any* age," Michael said, trying to make the case. "But, at your age, you're more vulnerable."

"That's ... that's *discrimination*," Pop said. "You're a racist!"

Michael held up his hands and cried out, "What if you were here alone—and had a choking fit?"

"I wouldn't be sitting alone at home with twenty lit birthday candles!" Pop said.

"Choking from something else," Michael countered.

Pop scowled. "I know what you're leading up to. So what if I really was choking? With you running around like the Three Stooges, I could have died surrounded by a crowd! Big deal. *Alone*, I might have stood a chance to survive."

Madison held up her phone. "Am I still calling 911?"

Pop shook his head. "See? I could have *walked* to the hospital in this amount of time. I don't need your or anyone else's help. *And I'm not moving out of my house!*"

Colleen stepped between Michael and Pop, holding a large and threatening-looking knife. "Let's cut the cake!"

Everyone went silent.

Elliot frowned at the cake. "With his spit all over it?"

The party didn't recover. Only Pop dared to eat a piece of cake. Colleen offered everyone ice cream, but an elderly man grumbled, "No, thanks. I don't know where it's been." Excuses were made, birthday cards were handed to Pop with handshakes and hugs, and then the house began to empty out.

Michael watched as the remaining guests scratched their heads and leaned to one another, asking if Michael was throwing Pop out of the house. If that's the case, a couple of people asked, could they have the old television sets? "I've had my eye on that Philco in the corner," said one old gent.

A few of them confessed quietly how they had noticed the changes in Pop's behavior over the past few months. They knew all along it would come to this.

Soon the only ones left were the Reynolds family, along with Aunt Minnie in her bunny rabbit outfit and Elliot. Elliot maintained a puzzled look on his face, even without a breadstick hanging from his lips.

"I hope you're satisfied," Pop finally said to Michael. He dropped into his easy chair again. "The whole town gets to see how my son treats his father on his birthday."

Michael gathered empty cups and put them on a tray. "I'm the bad guy? Your coughing fit was all my fault?"

"Nobody said you're a bad guy," Colleen said.

Michael put the tray on the dining table. "You're a horse doctor, Elliot. Tell him what they do with old horses. They're put out to pasture where someone can take care of them."

Elliot cleared his throat nervously. "Actually, we shoot them and send them to the glue factory."

Michael spun to him. "You actually do what?"

"Ha!" Pop said. "There's your answer. That's what you're planning."

Michael frowned at him. "We're not trying to shoot you and send you to a glue factory."

"You want to put me in a home," Pop said. "Same difference."

"Could we save this for tomorrow?" Colleen asked.

"I didn't bring it up," Michael said. But the urge to get the last word was too strong to resist. "I want to go on record to say that I am *not* an overreactor."

"Yes, you are," said Pop. "You always were—even when you were a kid. You worried and fretted and then turned into a basket case when things went wrong."

"Aunt Minnie, help me," Michael pleaded. "This isn't my doing."

Aunt Minnie pushed her bunny ears away from her face. "This is a family matter. Just tell me where to forward the mail."

"You *are* family—and it's because of your mail that we even started this discussion," Michael reminded her.

Aunt Minnie turned to Elliot. "I think it's time we went home."

"Now wait a minute," Michael said, moving toward her. "Don't throw me under the bus. Didn't you write to us that you were worried? Didn't you tell us about the visits to the doctor?"

Aunt Minnie's cheeks turned red. She stammered for a moment.

"Well, *Benedict* Minnie?" Pop asked with a steely gaze.

Aunt Minnie put on her coat. "I'm pleading the Fifth Amendment."

Michael couldn't let it go. "Please. Tell him he needs to move out of this house and get professional care before he hurts himself or someone else."

Pop was affronted. "Before I hurt someone else? I'm a danger to society now?"

"I'll clean up in the morning. Let's call it a night," Colleen suggested.

Pop glared at his son. "You see? You're overreacting again."

Michael reeled on him. "Tell me what happened to your car."

Pop looked at him with a blank expression.

"You've been in an accident," Michael said. "What happened?"

Pop looked away. "I don't know what you're talking about."

"My point exactly," Michael said. "You *don't* know. But there's a big dent in the fender. Is that an overreaction?"

"You're shouting, Dad," Madison said.

"Let's talk about this rationally. Like grown-ups," Aunt Minnie said as she adjusted the hips on her bunny costume.

"Please," Colleen appealed to them. "Let's not do this now, not tonight."

Michael held up his hands in a gesture of resignation. "But my father *wants to* talk about it now. Why do you think he's been jabbing at me all day? That's why he keeps pushing it."

"*I'm* pushing it?" Pop said. "Mr. Pot, meet Mr. Kettle! This is all you've thought about since you got here. From the minute you walked in the door, I knew what you were after. You wanted to talk me out of this house. That's how you are. It's how you've always been. You're pushy and bossy. Just ask anyone in this room."

"Now wait a minute," Michael said.

Pop cut him off. "Go on. Ask your family if you're pushy and bossy. You'll see."

"Okay, if that's what you want." Michael turned to his family. "Am I pushy and bossy?" He gestured to Colleen. "Well?"

"He's pushing your buttons, Michael," Colleen said quietly. "Don't you see?"

"Just humor him and answer the question. He said I'm overreacting and I'm pushy and bossy. Is he right?"

Colleen sighed. "Michael, stop. This isn't about you, remember?"

"That's not an answer," Pop said, wagging a finger at Michael as if he'd just scored a point somehow.

Michael was now pacing. He could feel the tension in his jaw, his teeth tightening and loosening, tightening and loosening. He was visibly trying to control his feelings.

"Ask Ethan," Pop said. "Ask *him* if you're pushy and bossy."

"This isn't about me," Michael said. "You want to talk about me, then we'll do that sometime. But right now—"

"No," Pop said firmly. "Go on, Ethan. Tell him the truth. Tell him how you really feel about college."

Ethan looked as if he wished the chair in which he was sitting would swallow him up.

Pop persisted. "Be a man, Ethan. Let him in on your little secret."

Michael turned to face Ethan. "What's he talking about?"

Ethan looked like a cornered mouse. "Well, sometimes you get locked into your own point of view and it's ... hard to talk to you when you get like that."

Michael gazed at his son. "And?"

"You have to realize that all these changes are ... are hard," Ethan said carefully. "And sometimes things aren't going to change the way you want them to."

"Tell me something I don't know, Ethan," Michael said. "Change can be hard. I know that. Change is scary. I'm scared about losing my future. I admit that. Why am I scared? Because I'm afraid I'll wind up wearing a paper hat and selling hamburgers at Biffy Barf's, answering to a kid your age. And Pop is scared of moving out of the house he's lived in for over forty years. Got it. The future is uncertain. I don't need you to tell me that."

"I'm not talking about your job or what's happening with Pop. I'm talking about other things." He swallowed hard.

"We're not talking about Madison getting a ring on her belly button," Michael said. "That's not going to happen."

"Leave me out of this," Madison said.

Michael took a step toward his son. "Be clear, Ethan. What are you talking about?"

"I've decided not to go back to college."

Colleen instinctively put a hand to her mouth. Madison lowered her face into her hands and groaned.

Aunt Minnie frowned at Pop. "Nice going, James."

"The boy needs to be honest with his father," Pop said simply.

Michael didn't take his eyes off of Ethan. "Really? No college? You've made that decision in favor of *what*, exactly?"

"I don't know. Not everybody plans everything out the way you do," Ethan said.

"There," Pop said, as if concluding his case. "Pushy, bossy ..."

Aunt Minnie gestured to Elliot. "We should be hopping along now. It's time for all old rabbits to be back to their dens."

"Can I go with you?" Madison asked.

Elliot went to the front door and grabbed the handle. He nodded back to everyone. "It was nice meeting you."

Aunt Minnie said, "Goodnight." She looked as if she had something else to say but changed her mind. The two left, tugging the door behind them.

Michael sat down on the couch. He felt as if he was being assaulted on two fronts. Working to find a calm tone, he said, "Ethan, you need a college degree to get anywhere. Even the computer tech companies require it."

"It's overrated, Dad," Ethan said. "The entrepreneurs rarely have degrees of any kind. They learn by experience."

Michael shook his head. "You're an entrepreneur? I'm sorry to break the news to you, son, but you inherited my lack of ambition. Remember? I couldn't even get you to open a lemonade stand on our street."

"I want to think about my life, decide what to do," Ethan said. "Maybe travel for a while."

"There's a solid plan." Michael scrubbed his face with his hands.

Ethan was on his feet. "Dad, can you think in terms of something other than a *solid plan*? Just once, can we allow for something that isn't a solid plan?"

"Not when it comes to your future, no."

"*My* future," Ethan snapped back. "It's *mine*, not yours."

"It's mine, too. Whatever you decide, I'll be the one to pick up the pieces."

Ethan stood behind a wingback chair, as if he needed it for cover. "This isn't something to argue about. I am eighteen. It's my decision. I'm laying off for a semester, maybe two, maybe more."

Michael folded his arms, pressing them down to restrain all that he wanted to say. "Fine. It's your decision. Good luck finding a job and a place to live."

Colleen had been piling dirty dishes and party debris on the dining table. She now turned. "Michael—" she began.

"I've always said the kids can live at home while they get their education. He's not doing that," Michael said, but he kept his eyes fixed on his son. "If you go to college, I'll do everything I can to help you. If you want to waste your time and *not* go to college, then you can't sponge off of me. It's that simple. I didn't work all these years to watch you throw it all away."

Ethan stared back at him, like a contest of wills. "I don't want anything from you. You can throw away your money however you want." He came out from behind the chair and went to the closet next to the front door. He reached in and pulled out his coat.

"Where are you going?" Colleen asked, alarmed.

"To get some fresh air," he answered. He fumbled with the buttons.

Michael watched him. There was something else to be said, but he didn't know how to say it. A line had been drawn. He couldn't erase it now.

Pop pushed himself up from his chair. "Now, now—there's no need to get overdramatic about this," he said. "Stick around, Ethan."

Ethan gave his grandfather a cold look. "Isn't this what you wanted? To divert the attention from you?"

Pop now looked worried, as if he realized he'd gone too far. "Michael, talk to your son." His voice had a slight tremble to it.

Michael was on his feet now, too. "What can I say without overreacting—or being pushy and bossy? Kudos, Dad. You've made your point."

Pop held up his hands. "Okay, I went too far. I do that sometimes. Your mother used to get after me about pushing your buttons. Remember? You and I would fight, and she always knew the right way to fix things right up."

"That's right, Dad. Joyful memories," Michael said sarcastically.

Pop lowered his head. He said softly, "I wish Laura could be here. She'd know what to do. She always did."

Michael cocked his head as if he hadn't heard right. "Laura?"

The change in Michael's tone seemed to catch Pop's attention. He looked up. "Yes. Laura."

"Laura *who*?" Michael asked.

"Your mother," Pop replied, looking as if Michael had just turned into a red canary.

"You mean *Linda*, don't you?" Michael asked.

Pop frowned at him. "I said Laura and I meant Laura. What's wrong with you?"

Michael glanced at his family. They all looked pale. Even Ethan, who hadn't left.

"What's wrong with everybody?" Pop asked, eyeing each of them.

Colleen said gently, "You meant to say Linda, I'm sure."

Pop gaped at her. "No, I didn't."

"Mom's name was *Linda*, not Laura," Michael said.

"You're crazy," Pop said. But Michael saw the shadow of doubt cross his face.

"Where's that stuff we brought down from the attic?" Michael asked. "The framed marriage certificate."

It was sitting on a table nearest to Madison. She handed it over.

Michael took a quick look, then gave it to his father.

Pop wouldn't look at the certificate at first. "I don't need to see that."

"Linda," Pop whispered. He was looking at the certificate now. His face had fallen. He shook his head. His voice shook as he said, "I'm looking right at her name, but it … it's not familiar."

"That happens to me in geometry all the time," Madison said with a grim smile.

Pop headed for the kitchen and said, "I'm going to tidy up now."

"I'll do it," Colleen offered.

"No," Pop said firmly. "I want to."

Michael watched as Pop walked to the kitchen.

Ethan pushed open the storm door. Cool autumn air poured in. "I'm going out," he said.

Michael looked helplessly at his son. Ethan stepped out and closed the door.

Chapter 5

Pop carried half-empty cups of punch and crumb-covered paper plates to the wastebasket in the kitchen. He had to bite his lower lip to keep from talking to himself, a habit he'd formed while living alone for such a long time. The family had gone upstairs.

Now he wished he hadn't insisted on cleaning up. After only a few trips between the kitchen and the living room, he felt tired, ready for bed. He thought he'd like to crawl under the covers and read himself to sleep. He was in the middle of a Zane Grey book. *East of Eden?* No, that was Steinbeck. What was it called? He couldn't think of the name.

He worked to fight off a growing sense of panic. Tired ... forgetful ... exactly what Dr. Janssen had warned him would happen. How many times had he gone to the store for milk and come back with something other than milk? Or he'd gone out for bread, thought he'd forgotten it, bought some more, then returned home to a cabinet full of bread. It had been happening a lot lately. He didn't dare tell anyone about the stack of unpaid bills he'd shoved in his dresser drawer. It wasn't that he lacked the money to pay them, but that writing checks had become so difficult. He couldn't remember which way a seven turned, or which line was for numbers and which line was for his signature.

Michael had brought up Pop's car accident, but what Michael didn't know was that Pop had stopped driving a long time ago. Not because of the accident. That was stupid. He'd backed into a guard rail somewhere. The stupid part was that he'd parked the car halfway in and halfway out of the garage to bring in some groceries from the trunk and misplaced the keys. Maybe he'd locked them in the trunk. He wasn't sure. And he couldn't find the extra set to check. At some point, he'd have to tell his son. A new set of keys would have to be made. The thought added to a surge of anger that had been building all day.

Until the end, he thought he'd done well at the party. Michael and Colleen could never have guessed how traumatized he was at the thought of all those people coming over. He had stood in the bathroom beforehand and considered different ways to get out of it. Standing with his hands clenching the side of the sink, he had wanted to lock the door and not let anyone into his house. Then he felt the gathering warmth around his crotch and the cool sting down his legs and he realized he'd wet himself. He had to do a fast change-of-clothes, including an adult diaper. He prayed no one would notice.

Michael saved the day without even knowing it. Talking about moving out of the house gave him something to focus his anger on.

Pop now shoved everything into the wastebasket and then, almost instinctively, dug into the trash to pull out some silverware. He'd been doing a lot of that lately, too.

It was the *big* mistake that preyed on his mind. How could he confuse Linda's name with Laura? *Laura!* Did he know any

Lauras? He'd never dated one. But the name was fixed there in his memory. Tragic. Linda was the one person in his life that he couldn't forget. There wasn't a minute in any hour of any day when he didn't think about her. Sometimes he prayed that God would let her visit him—just let him see her every once in a while. She didn't even have to talk, though he talked to her often enough whether she was there or not.

Even now, as he went back to the living room, he chatted with her. *This is what you missed by leaving too soon*, he said. To think that he could look her in the face and not know her name. *What would you say? What would you say if you found me trying to shovel snow that wasn't there?* Perhaps he could cope with all those things if she were with him. He wasn't supposed to grow old without her. Some days he resented her for leaving him behind to face his life alone.

But you're not alone, she would say. *God saw you through your youth and he will see you through your old age. You must have faith.*

Easy for you to say, Pop argued. *You're not dealing with it.*

Pop was disappointed. What had happened to the wise elder he thought he'd be? Once upon a time he'd envisaged himself as a white-haired sage who would have people knocking on his door for advice every day. *They knocked on my door, all right. And asked me to give up my Sunday school class.*

Why was this happening to him? Was it something he did wrong as a young man? He'd lived a clean life, hadn't he? No cussing, no tobacco, only a little alcohol, no gambling, no philandering. Maybe he *should* have messed with all those things, then he would have died at the age of fifty and not have had to worry about this. Was this the end of a righteous life? Was this God's reward: slowly going through his body, like an old house, and turning off the lights one at a time?

Pop looked around him. He was sitting in his favorite chair, but he couldn't remember when he had sat down. Had he been asleep? He'd come into the living room but couldn't remember now why he was there.

A blast of cool air covered him. He thought he heard rain. Then he realized that someone had opened the front door. Ethan stepped in, quietly closed the door, hung up his coat in the closet, and headed for the stairs.

He doesn't know I'm here, Pop thought. *Maybe I'm not. Maybe I've disappeared.*

But Ethan suddenly stopped at the foot of the stairs and tipped his head. "Pop?"

"Hi, Ethan."

"Why are you sitting in the dark?"

Pop had to look around. He hadn't realized he was sitting in the dark. "I was just thinking. What time is it?"

"Two fifteen."

"Don't *you* start."

"It is!" Ethan tried to show him the face of his watch by the light of the stairs on the landing.

"Where've you been?" Pop asked.

"Walking around," Ethan replied. "I never realized how quiet a town could be in the middle of the night. The all-night diner on Main Street was open, though."

"I don't know how they stay in business." Pop remembered when they built the diner some sixty years ago. That was back when Hope Springs did a strong business with travelers in the summer—people using the main road on their way to somewhere, or on their way back. There was the diner and a couple of motels. Now there was just the diner.

"Everything's changing, Pop."

Pop nodded sadly. "Awfully fast."

Ethan sat down on the couch, a shadow. Pop could almost imagine him as a little boy again. "Change isn't always bad, though," Ethan said.

"No, I don't suppose it is."

"I've been doing a lot of thinking."

"About what?" Pop asked.

"Everything," Ethan replied. "Mostly about moving, though."

"Ah. Moving." He said the word distastefully.

"People move out of comfortable situations and are very happy," Ethan reasoned.

Pop squinted at his grandson. He was still a shadow on the couch, but Pop thought he could make out the whites of his eyes and teeth. "Are they happy?" Pop asked.

"Sure," Ethan said. "In fact, some people say that if you live too comfortably, you'll stop growing. You become stagnant."

"Who says that?" Pop asked. Words like *growing* and *stagnant* were the stuff of pop psychologists, business gurus, and advertising writers. Pop didn't trust any of them. "Living comfortably isn't such a bad thing, is it?"

"Maybe not," Ethan said, a hint of worry in his voice. "But people say it. You know. The people who say those kinds of things."

Pop scrubbed his chin. "They're not always right, you know."

"I know. But they might be this time," Ethan pushed a hand through his curly hair. "Growth involves change, doesn't it?"

And pain, Pop thought. *Sometimes it involves a lot of pain.*

Ethan spoke as if he'd come to a decision. "But we have to swallow our pride and push ahead."

Pop thought about Linda again. What would she say to him now? *You have to step ahead in faith, James, and believe that God will see you through.* That's what it was all about, right?

"Pop?"

"We have to step ahead in faith. God will see us through," Pop said, an echo of the thoughts in his head. He didn't feel the truth of the words, but he believed them.

"That's right," Ethan said. He stood up. His voice took on a sense of urgency and passion that Pop recognized as hallmarks of youth. "I mean, you've gotta change or you'll stop growing. Otherwise, you might as well be dead. I'm not dead. Are you?"

"I'm afraid to check. But, no, I don't think so."

"Then we have to accept change," Ethan concluded.

Pop nodded. "I guess we do."

"Fine." Pop could hear him settle back down onto the couch. "That settles it, then."

"I guess it does," Pop said with a twinge of sadness. And there it was. The decision was made. "But what about you, Ethan? Have you done any thinking about what you're going to do?"

Ethan paused, then he sounded confused when he said, "That's what I've been talking about. I'm moving out of the house while I figure out what I'm going to do with my life."

"Oh," Pop said, shaking his head. He'd gotten their conversation mixed up.

Ethan still didn't get it. "What did you think we were talking about, Pop?"

"I'm talking about moving out of my house and going to one of those retirement places."

Ethan chuckled. "Oh."

Pop chuckled, too, but felt there was no humor in it. He hoped Linda was watching from somewhere, pleased with his decision.

Ethan leaned forward and asked, "Are you sure?"

"Are *you* sure?" Pop challenged him, as if Ethan's answer affected his own.

"Yes," Ethan replied firmly.

Pop nodded. "Then so am I."

PART TWO

CHRISTMAS AT THE FADED FLOWER

Chapter 6

Pop had moved into his Faded Flower apartment a month after his birthday party. He had lost his strength to fight the inevitable, especially after all those tests in Denver. The big guns. Brain scans, body scans, cognitive tests, memory ... it was worse than he could have imagined. By the end, how could he fight the data—the diagnoses—that his brain had always been a windup clock that was now winding down? *Alzheimer's*. No matter how angry it made him, he couldn't argue with the doctors. That was it. Michael had his victory.

No—that was unfair. Michael never acted like he was pleased to be right. Just the opposite. He looked sadder than ever, wearing the face of a man who seemed both burdened and bewildered.

A steady determination was what Michael exuded as they met with the doctors, then that lawyer fellow to sort out the will and power of attorney and all the bureaucratic forms that had to be handled. Pop bristled. But Colleen was the one who gently reminded him of all the problems that would happen if he didn't prepare now for the future. And his pensions and retirement and Medicare had to be sorted out. Dennis gave long-distance advice, as usual. They needed his expertise. Living in a retirement center wouldn't be cheap.

They talked about selling his house. But Michael wondered aloud if more money would be made from selling the house in Denver first. He hadn't found a job in the Denver area. And, these days, so many people worked from home. The family could temporarily live in Pop's house in Hope Springs.

Good. It stays in the family, Pop had thought. *And I don't have to downsize yet.*

The apartment was a simple two-room-and-a-bathroom setup. It had a living room and basic kitchen area, a bedroom and walk-in closet, and the bathroom. The Faded Flower offered three meals a day, with coffee, tea, and ice cream available in the Dining Room around the clock. There were events and games scheduled at certain times on various days, most of them taking place in the Recreation Room.

The Faded Flower itself wasn't a conventional-looking retirement home. Pop learned that it was once the Grayson Mansion— a sprawling Victorian-type house that had been renovated, expanded, and stretched to accommodate the elderly with a variety of needs. One wing was set up with modest apartments for retirees, another wing offered more intensive physical care and rehabilitation, yet another focused on those with dementia and Alzheimer's. Pop knew he would wind up there eventually. In the meantime, everything was contrived to evoke a cozy homelike atmosphere. For the most part, it succeeded. Over the past couple of weeks, the Christmas decorations went up all over the building. Garland, artificial pine with snow-covered needles, red ribbons, and tinsel appeared on the walls, above the doorways, and on the dark wood shelves that had been strategically placed in the various common rooms. A giant

Christmas tree was placed in the foyer. Fake, of course, to avoid lawsuits over any allergies to real pine.

The staff were friendly, sometimes a little condescending— talking to the residents like small children. Though, Pop had to admit that a few of his neighbors acted like they had regressed to the age of four. Christmas seemed to bring it out all the more in a few people.

Today was Christmas Eve and Pop had made his way to the Sun Room—a recreation room with a quadrangle of glass that faced west and caught the afternoon sun. The rest of the room had a mix of tables and chairs, oversized pictures painted in a kind of Italian style, a large bulletin board designated for personal snapshots, and a wall dedicated to framed photos of the veterans in the facility. A piano sat on one wall, with a sign above it stating "No Piano Playing Allowed After 7 P.M."

For the holiday season, someone had hung red and green tissue paper decorations from the ceiling, draping them from the corners to meet a giant red bell in the middle of the ceiling. Cardboard cutout letters saying "Merry Christmas" were stretched along one wall. On a conference table in the corner, a small artificial tree was half decorated with silver and gold balls. Next to it sat a punch bowl, coffee maker, and paper cups.

Pop had walked in just as a woman named Libby was pushing a wheelchair holding a surly creature named Ethel.

"Take me back!" Ethel was demanding. "I want to go back to my room." Then she shouted, "Help! Nurse! A madwoman is trying to kidnap me!"

Libby caught Pop's gaze and rolled her eyes. "Don't be so stubborn, Ethel. You don't want to spend Christmas Eve alone in your room, do you?"

"Yes!" Ethel snapped. She shouted again, "Nurse!"

"I don't believe you and I won't let you. The people from the church are coming to sing for us, and if we don't make a good showing, they might not come back."

"Suits me!" Ethel said. "I don't care if they come back. I want to be left alone. Now take me back!"

Libby found a spot near one of the tables and parked Ethel at the end. She reached down and fixed the brake into position. "You're staying right here."

"If I could walk, you wouldn't get away with this," Ethel said.

"But you can't and you're staying put," Libby said firmly. She was a short, plump woman with cropped gray hair, humor-filled eyes, and a friendly strength that brought order to the other residents' natural disorder. Though she was also a resident, she had become a caretaker to everyone around her. She added, "And don't try to wheel yourself out because I'll catch you before you get to the door."

Ethel scowled at her. "I wish I had one of those *motorized* chairs. Then I could run you over,"

Libby laughed. "You don't mean that."

"Just try me."

Libby went to the table with the half-decorated tree. Reaching under the table, she brought out a box of ornaments and busied herself unpacking them.

Ethel glanced over at Pop. "She is a wicked, wicked woman. She dragged me in here against my will."

Pop still felt like a newcomer, so he limited his response to a friendly smile as he went to the coffee maker and poured himself a small cup.

Just then, a woman named Maggie walked in. She had short-cropped white hair and smiling blue eyes. She wore a dark overcoat and carried a small purse, looking as if she was going out for the evening.

"Maggie!" Ethel cried. "Call the police. Call my lawyer. This is elderly abuse."

Maggie smiled. "Now, Ethel, I'm sure that if Libby brought you here, it's for your own good."

"It's not. She wants me to have a heart attack so she can take my TV." She called out to Libby, "You're not in my will, Libby. You won't get it."

"I'm glad to hear you have a will," Maggie said.

"I don't," Ethel countered. "But I'll write one, put her in it, and then take her out again just to teach her a lesson."

Maggie turned her attention to Pop. "How are you, James?" she asked him.

Pop sipped his coffee and said, "Better than some." He asked Libby, "Do we know when the church group will be here?"

"Church group! Ha!" Ethel said. "It'll be five losers who have nothing better to do. Why else would they want to spend Christmas Eve with us, talking about our arthritis or our irregularity or the friends we buried or reminiscing about times they can't possibly know about ...?"

She's not entirely wrong, Pop thought.

Libby ignored her. "They could get here any time after six."

Pop wondered who would actually come. Over the past couple of weeks, folks from the various churches had sent some groups in to do concerts or lead in some Christmas carol singing. The Baptists were particularly good. The Lutherans were very serious.

The Episcopalians tried to be hip, blending songs like "White Christmas" with "O Holy Night," led by a man with a long ponytail. (Pop assumed it was a man but could never be sure.) St. Clare's Catholic Church was slotted to come that evening. Catholics weren't known for their concerts and sing-alongs, so he didn't know what to expect. This was his first Christmas in a retirement center.

"How do you feel?" Libby asked Maggie.

"Better," Maggie replied. "Spending Christmas Eve with my son and his family is the best medicine for me."

"When will you be back?"

"Tomorrow mid-day." Maggie gave her a knowing smile. "We'll open presents together, then they're going to *her* mother's house for dinner."

"You aren't going?" asked Libby.

"I was invited."

Libby nodded. "I'm glad you'll be here for part of Christmas Day."

Maggie touched Libby's arm. "It wouldn't be Christmas if I couldn't spend part of it with you."

Ethel began to make a retching noise. "Will you two hurry up and say goodbye? You're making me ill."

"Hush, Ethel," Libby said.

The two women hugged and wished each other a Merry Christmas.

Maggie walked to the door but stopped when Libby said, "Don't forget: no sweets."

Maggie turned. "I won't forget."

Libby smiled at her. "You won't forget until those homemade cookies are out of the oven."

Maggie shook her head. "My daughter-in-law doesn't know how to make homemade cookies. She has no patience with anything that isn't pre-made from the store."

"Then teach her," Libby suggested.

Maggie lifted a cautionary eyebrow. "That would be intrusive." She drew her coat around her. "Merry Christmas, Libby. You, too, James."

"Merry Christmas," Pop said to her.

She gave a slight bow to Ethel. "Good night, Ethel."

"Drop me off at my room on the way out, will you, Maggie?" Ethel asked, all innocence.

Maggie laughed, a light musical sound, as she left the room.

Ethel snorted. "I don't know why everyone makes such a fuss over Christmas. It's always so cold."

"Not in the heart, Ethel. It's the birth of our Savior," Libby said cheerfully.

"*Yours*, maybe," Ethel said.

More of the residents began to drift into the room. Pop looked at the gathering crowd and wondered why he was among them. Some were stoop-shouldered, some wrapped their gnarled hands around the bars of their walkers and moved in a slow shuffle, some had looks of constant confusion on their faces. What was he doing here with all these old people?

An exceptionally dapper gentleman named Henry arrived. He had iron-gray hair and a nearly perfect face; even his wrinkles looked strategically placed. He walked with the stride of someone half his age and was an incorrigible flirt, getting a slight girlish blush from Ethel when he kissed her on the top of the head. He called her a "cantankerous old blossom" and thanked her for coming to the evening's festivities.

Ethel grumbled, "I had no choice. Beelzebub over there made me." She nodded to Libby.

"She did that for me!" Henry exclaimed. "I told her that I wouldn't come unless you were here."

"Liar," Ethel said. "The only reason you're here is because your family stood you up. Right?"

Henry gave her a disapproving look. "They did not 'stand me up,' as you say. The weather people are calling for snow tonight. I decided that the weather was too dangerous for her to drive all this way and told them not to come."

Ethel persisted. "You said that *after* they made other plans. A party, wasn't it? Stacy told me all about it."

"Stacy shouldn't be eavesdropping." Pop thought he heard a crack in Henry's carefully constructed charm.

"No better time to *eaves*drop than Christmas *Eve*," Ethel said and threw herself into a coughing fit by laughing at her own poor joke.

Henry sauntered over to Libby, still at the tree table, and assisted her with the making of a fresh bowl of punch. Libby asked him if he would go find someone called David. "He's probably gotten lost again." Henry said he would and seemed to glide out of the room.

Pop made his way to a cushioned chair off to the side, feeling like the new kid at school, unsure of his place in the room or with these people. He had chatted with them amiably enough at mealtimes and on the rare occasions when he went to one of the special events or games. But his ability to remember names, faces, and personal details often left him drained. As he strolled across the room, a short, gray-haired woman came through the door. She wore a pillbox-style hat and a heavy coat. She pulled a wheeled suitcase behind her.

"Where are you going, Lillian?" Libby asked, drawing close and giving her a gentle hug.

Lillian beamed. "Home. I told you this afternoon, remember?" She sat down in a chair near the door, clasping her hands on her lap. She looked like someone waiting for a bus.

Libby tried to mask a look of concern that shadowed her face. "You're going *home*?"

"Yes. Ben is coming to get me. He wrote me a letter telling me so."

Libby carefully said, "He's coming here to pick you up? Tonight? He said so in a letter?"

Lillian gave an enthusiastic nod.

"I would love to see that letter," Libby said. "Do you have it nearby?"

Lillian said, "Well, yes. It's ..." She began digging in her various pockets. Then she drew out a crumpled envelope. "Here it is."

Libby took the envelope and pulled out the letter inside. She then gave Pop a forlorn look. "Lillian, this letter was written several years ago. Remember? Ben didn't come. He hasn't come. I don't think he will."

"This place is a loony bin," Ethel said. She'd been watching them.

Libby gestured for her to be quiet. "Why don't you take your coat off, Lillian? We're going to have a very special Christmas program that I think you'll enjoy."

"No, thank you. I want to be ready for Ben."

Libby reached for Lillian's collar and gave a slight tug. "You'll get too hot in here and chilled when you go out. You don't want to get a chill, do you?"

"Well. No, now that you mention it." And with that, Lillian allowed Libby to help her out of her coat.

Pop watched them, appreciative of Libby's tenderness. He didn't know much about Lillian or who Ben was, but he had his suspicions.

"Merry Christmas, my dears!" came a joyful cry from a single door on the opposite wall. It was a beanpole of a woman named Veronica. She had large dark eyes, bright red lips, and cheekbones you could cut bread with. A shock of white hair stood straight up like the bride of Frankenstein. However, unlike her, Veronica was a genuinely kind woman, eccentric and flamboyant to the core. She now carried a basket of roses and moved around the room handing one to each of the residents with sweeping gestures. "Flowers to all! Paul Newman used to give all his friends flowers on Christmas Eve. He threw the most divine Christmas bashes. Music and dramatic sketches and dancing until midnight. Robert Redford put his feet in the punch bowl once. I laughed until I cried. Sean Connery wrote a memoir about it. Or was it Burt Reynolds? One of them did. Both had a crush on me, you know."

Pop was warned that Veronica had a memory that may have been more imagination than reality. She claimed to have been a popular actress once, but no one could find any proof of her career, apart from bit parts in a few Broadway plays and East Coast–based movies and television. All back in the 1960s. It was said that she had come to Colorado to film a Western but was abandoned without money when the production suddenly folded.

"Where are the singers?" Veronica asked. "Is there not to be a show tonight? Neil Simon once said to me—"

"Veronica, would you stir the punch, please?" Libby asked, distracting her from whatever Neil Simon had once said.

"Of course, my dear," she said.

"Take Ethel back to her room," Ethel commanded.

Veronica smiled and moved behind Ethel's wheelchair.

Libby caught Veronica's arm and said, "You were going to stir the punch for me."

"Oh, yes," Veronica said and shifted to the punch bowl.

Ethel glowered at Libby.

Pop was beginning to find this group of people more entertaining than anything he might have watched on television in his apartment. And, just as he had that thought, a voice contradicted it.

"Not here! I want to watch 'Mr. Magoo's Christmas Carol.' It's on TV!"

Pop's attention went to the main double doors. Henry was leading David in by the arm.

"You can watch Mr. Magoo anytime. You have the videotape. I've seen it in your room. Besides, it's Christmas Eve."

"Christmas Eve! Then I wanna watch Dick Clark. I love Dick Clark."

"That's New Year's Eve, David. And, besides, Dick Clark is dead."

"Every band leader has his ups and downs," David said. "You watch. Two years from now and he'll be popular again." David saw Lillian sitting with her suitcase. "Hello, Lillian."

"Hello, David."

"Any sign of Ben yet?" David asked.

"Not yet. But I'm sure he'll be here soon."

Veronica called out, "Where's Frederick? Frederick's not here! We can't do this without Frederick!"

"Frederick can't come," said Henry.

"Why not?"

"He's gone to be with the Lord," Henry explained.

Veronica looked relieved. "Oh, good. I was afraid he had died."

Ethel snarled and banged her hands on the arm rest of her wheelchair. "Listen to how we talk! 'He passed away.' 'He's gone to be with the Lord.' Why don't we just call a spade a spade and say what it is?"

"I don't think this is appropriate talk for Christmas Eve," Veronica said.

"Oh, *pooh*," Ethel said. "What makes Christmas Eve any different?"

"The birthday of Jesus is a time for beginnings, not endings," Libby said. "And that makes it a time to celebrate, not go on and on about death."

"Pooh," said Ethel.

Henry said, "I'll tell you what, Ethel: we can talk about death on *your* birthday."

"With any luck, I won't be here for my next birthday."

Henry smiled at her. "That'll give us a better reason to talk about it."

Veronica waved at them impatiently. "Enough of this jibber-jabber. I want to sing." She moved to the center of the room and began to attack "Deck the Halls" but soon got lost in all the *fa-la-la-la-las*.

"Now, Veronica," Libby said, sliding an arm through hers, "you know what the doctor said about your singing."

Veronica looked at her defensively. "He didn't say it was bad for me."

"True. He said it was bad for everyone else." A few chuckled as Libby led Veronica to the snack table.

As the newcomer to the Faded Flower, Pop had to wonder if this was a scene these people played out every Christmas. Maybe it was being played out in old folks' homes all over the country. Lonely people trying to mask their loneliness. He was thankful that Michael and his family were nearby.

Pop sat to the side like a mere observer. It was the unfamiliarity of it all that made him want to withdraw. This room, these people, another world. Even his own apartment intimidated him in the smallest of ways. Favorite plates and mugs were there, but they were tucked in different cabinets. His clothes hung on hangers in closets that were not his own. In the morning, his feet touched a floor that belonged to someone else. The smells were foreign. He felt as if he'd become a stranger to his life.

These were the thoughts he was having when a woman wearing a red dress and green sweater shot into the room. It was Becky Garcia—or *Miss* Garcia, as they called her. She was an events coordinator for the center, a bundle of crackling energy and enthusiasm. "Ladies and gentlemen," she said, "before they go home, a few members of the day crew would like to wish you a Merry Christmas."

She stepped aside and a few nurses, orderlies, and other staff members came in. Wearing the center's uniform blue polo shirts, they had wrapped festive-colored scarves around their necks. They looked at each other awkwardly until one of them started singing "We Wish You a Merry Christmas."

Pop hadn't realized that the song had so many verses. First, the singers demanded to be brought figgy pudding, then they said they wouldn't go until they got some, then they admitted that they really *like* their figgy pudding—and the whole time Pop was trying to remember what figgy pudding actually was. The singers eventually came to a rousing finish. Instead of getting figgy pudding, Libby presented them with chocolate chip cookies.

After scattered applause and with waves and Merry Christmases, the day shift made their way out. Pop watched as Ethel, seeing an opportunity, began to wheel herself with them.

Libby caught her in time and pulled her back to the table. "Ah-ah-ah. Not so fast."

"Rats," Ethel said.

Miss Garcia announced that the church group should be arriving soon. "I'll be at the reception desk if you need anything," she said.

Lillian looked up at her. "Has Ben arrived yet?"

"Ben? No. I'm sorry, Lillian."

Lillian gave a small shrug. "He's always late for everything."

"About five years late," Ethel murmured.

Pop was about to stand up to get another cup of coffee when David dropped down next to him.

"Gordon," David said.

"I'm Jim," said Pop.

"I know," David said. "I'm talking about Gordon."

"Who's Gordon?" Pop asked.

"You know. The gardener." David looked around as if he didn't want to be overheard. "Gordon was trimming the bushes outside of my window."

"Oh."

"Six forty-five *every* morning."

"Your bushes grow that fast?" Pop asked. "He has to trim them *every* morning?"

David's eyes grew wide with an *Isn't it amazing?* expression. "Every morning. It's enough to wake the dead."

"I hope not. The last thing I want is a visit from my mother," Pop joked.

David turned to face him. "Your mother's coming to visit?"

"Heavens no. My mother is dead. Twenty-five—no, *twenty-eight*—years now."

"That's awfully young for a mother to die."

"Not her age," Pop explained. "That's how long she's been dead."

"So, who raised you? Your father? Alone?"

"Raised me?" Pop asked.

David continued, "Some maiden aunts? A pack of wolves?"

Pop looked at him, bewildered. "My father and mother raised me."

"Your *mother*? What was she—a ghost? I don't understand."

Pop realized the source of David's confusion and said, "See, *you* said, 'It's enough to wake the dead,' and I said, as a joke, that ..."

David had a vacant expression.

Pop surrendered.

◆

There was a flurry of excitement when a young man—Pop thought he was probably Ethan's age—came into the room. He was tall with curly hair and a lean face. He looked around the room, then went to Libby and said, "Grandma?"

Libby looked surprised. "Sorry, I'm not your grandmother. I've never seen you before."

The young man seemed equally surprised. "You're not? Are you sure?"

"Of course I'm sure."

The young man looked around the room, embarrassed. "Then which one of you is my grandmother? The woman at the front said you're here." He eyed the room, his gaze falling on Pop.

"It certainly isn't *me*," Pop said.

Ethel shook her head. "The boy doesn't know his own grandmother?"

"Well, at this age, we do all look alike," Henry said.

"What kind of grandson would forget what his grandmother looks like?" Ethel complained.

"What kind of grandmother is forgetting what her grandson looks like," Pop observed.

The young man began to dig into his jeans' pockets. "I haven't seen her since I was little. All I have is a ..." He kept digging until he brought out a phone. "A picture! I have a picture!" He thumbed at the screen.

Slowly, moving like zombies from a horror movie, the residents gathered around him to look. Even Pop stood up and went to see.

The picture was actually a photo of a framed black-and-white portrait from years ago. Pop thought the face was familiar. Then, almost as one, everyone looked from the screen and over to the one person who hadn't joined them.

"No," Ethel said. She looked stricken.

"Grandma!" the young man shouted and went over to her for a hug.

Ethel backed away. "No! It's a mistake!"

He hugged her anyway.

"Stop it! I don't even know you!" she cried.

"But I'm your grandson!"

"How am I supposed to know that?" Ethel said, pushing him away. "Whose boy are you?"

"My dad is Leonard. Your son."

"Ha! Leonard!" Ethel said. She looked around her, as if she'd lost something. "Where's my purse? If you're Leonard's son, I want to keep an eye on my purse."

"Ethel!" Libby snapped.

Ethel gave the young man a hard look. "Why are you here? What do you want? You want money for school, don't you? You are in school, am I right?"

"Yes, but—"

"I knew it! Leonard sent you for school money!"

"He didn't. In fact, he doesn't even know I'm here," the young man said.

"Oh?"

"I'm driving home for Christmas. He's not expecting me until tomorrow. Since my university is only a couple of hours from here, I decided to come and see you first."

"I don't trust you. You never came to visit me before. Nobody has. Why now?"

"Because you're my grandmother."

"That never meant anything to anyone before."

"It does to me."

Ethel gave him a long look. Pop couldn't tell if she was touched or suspicious. "I remember you now. *Richard*. You were the one that always jumped in my lap first thing when you came to visit. You destroyed my knees. In fact, it's probably your fault I'm in this wheelchair."

Richard seemed unsure about how to respond. "I'm sorry," he said.

"You're ... you're all grown up," Ethel said. "Not a bad looker, considering you're Leonard's son. Thank God you didn't inherit his big ears."

Miss Garcia came to the doorway and announced that the people from St. Clare's had arrived. As she was speaking, Father Cliff Montgomery, the young priest who pastored the church, walked in. Pop liked Father Cliff. Since moving into the Faded Flower, Pop had been visited several times by the priest, who often asked his advice about parish matters. It was a consolation prize, as if Father Cliff was saying, *You may not be able to teach the catechists, but you can teach me.*

"Sorry we're late," Father Cliff said. "We had some confusion about the time."

David, who had fallen asleep in the chair next to Pop, came awake. "Is it time for Dick Clark? Has the ball dropped in Times Square?"

"That's New Year's Eve, David," Pop said, marveling that David could be so fixated on the wrong holiday. "It's *Christmas* Eve. Some folks from St. Clare's are here to sing for us."

"Is Dick Clark with them? Did he bring his banjo?"

"Banjo?" Pop asked, then realized David's mistake. "You're thinking of Roy Clark from 'Hee Haw.'"

"What? No. He didn't play banjo. He played guitar and sat on that horse of his. The one called Trigger."

Pop gazed at David. "That's *Roy Rogers*."

David shook his head. "What's wrong with you? She was Fred Astaire's dance partner."

"Ginger Rogers," Pop said, feeling routed.

"She didn't do Westerns," David said. "It'd be too hard to dance wearing spurs!"

Pop wondered what kind of meds David had forgotten to take.

Miss Garcia began to herd the residents to the tables and chairs. As she did that, Father Cliff handed out sheets of paper with lyrics to Christmas carols and hymns. While that happened, a dozen people in overcoats and scarves came in. Pop saw Colleen and Madison mixed in the crowd. They smiled at him. He waved.

Miss Garcia guided the group to an open area nearest the piano. A man sat on the bench and began to play while the singers organized themselves.

Pop found himself near Ethel and her grandson. Richard sat with an awkward look, unsure of what to do with this grandmother he'd come to see, but who didn't seem interested in him.

The piano man struck up the first notes of "Joy to the World" and the singing started. Some of the residents joined in, a few just mouthed the words. A couple of them—including Ethel—watched as if it was an endurance test. The ensemble sounded better than Pop had expected, even harmonizing without losing their way.

Pop sang along, hoping that the familiarity of the songs would ease the unfamiliarity of the setting.

Interspersed with the music, Father Cliff read passages from St. Matthew's and St. Luke's accounts of the birth of Jesus.

The program—if it was actually a program—lasted almost forty-five minutes and wrapped up with a few last words from Father Cliff about the true meaning of Christmas. Miss Garcia then invited them to mix and mingle for a while.

Colleen brought Pop a cup of punch. She sat on one side of him. Madison sat down on the other side, pulling him close for a kiss on the cheek. "It's starting to snow," she said and looked pleased to tell him the news.

"Where is your father?" Pop asked her.

"Home, waiting for Ethan to get here from Denver. Traffic is bad, I guess."

Ethan had been keeping an eye on the house in Denver while Michael, Colleen, and Madison drove back and forth between the city and Hope Springs.

"We'll pick you up later for Midnight Mass," Colleen said. "Are you sure you want to stay up for that?"

"I'm sure."

"Then we'll take you home and wake up to a wonderful Christmas tomorrow."

Pop smiled and nodded. "I'm sure it will be."

The piano man launched into a song that Pop recognized from "A Charlie Brown Christmas."

"It's time to go," Colleen said. "We're going to stop by the hospital to sing. Then we have to get Father Cliff back to the church in time for the nine o'clock Mass."

Colleen and Madison hugged him and then joined the exodus from the room.

Pop sat for a moment, feeling the loss. He heard Richard venture to ask Ethel, "So, how are you, Grandma?"

"How do I look?" she asked. It was a challenge.

"You look ... great."

"You're a liar just like your father," Ethel snapped. "Where's my purse?"

"Are they treating you well here?" he asked. "This seems like a nice place."

Ethel snorted. "Easy for you to say. You're allowed to leave."

"You don't like it here?" he asked.

"No!"

"Why not?"

"Because it's crowded and stuffy and everyone knows everyone else's business and nobody will leave me alone." Ethel gestured to the room. "And it's full of a bunch of old people. I don't like old people."

"But you're old," he said.

"That's why I don't like them," Ethel said. Pop watched her lean close to Richard. "They torture me here, you know," she said.

Richard looked at her, aghast. Pop put a hand over his mouth to hide his smile.

"They beat me if I don't do what they say," she continued. "They perform illegal operations on the brain and do all kinds of shock treatments."

"Are you serious?" Richard asked.

"I've had so many shock treatments they could use me as a Christmas tree," she said. She pointed to Libby. "See her? She's the gestapo around here. She'll snitch on you in a minute for brownie points and get her electric blanket turned up a notch or two. You've got to get me out of here, Robert."

"Richard."

Pop made eye contact with the young man and shook his head. "She's teasing you," Pop said.

"Mind your own business," Ethel said. She turned to Richard. "He's the new guy. They brought him in because of his skill to beat people with rubber hoses and not leave any marks."

"And waterboarding with bedpans," Pop added. He asked Ethel, "Can't you just relax and enjoy the season?"

"Pooh on the season," Ethel said. "All the season does is remind me that I'm old and lonely. I don't need the season. It's full of false hopes. I think it's a cruel trick to dangle the birth of Jesus in our faces as if it has the power to make the pain from the rest of the year go away."

"But this young man has come all this way to see you," Pop said. He felt the first churnings of anger in his gut.

Ethel looked disdainfully at Richard. "He wants money. I can tell."

Richard stood up. "Maybe it was a mistake," he said. "I'll go." He grabbed his coat from the back of the chair. As he put it on, he said to her, "I'm not here for your money. I don't want anything from you. I know you've been alone here for a long time and that my family has neglected you. I'm sorry. I have no excuse. But I want that to change. I want to come see you more, to make up for the time I've been your grandchild and haven't acted like it. I want to visit more often."

Pop was impressed. He looked down at his cup of coffee and wondered what Ethel would say. She didn't waste any time.

"Just like your father," she said. "A good talker. But understand this, young man: good talk, promises, occasional notes and cards don't replace flesh and blood."

Pop looked up at her just as she pointed to Lillian, sitting with her suitcase.

"See her? She's waiting for family who have never come and never will. People think she's pathetic. They think she's senile. Well, I'm not senile, and I'm not waiting for anyone. So keep your promises and your false hopes to yourself. I'm not interested." She turned away from her grandson and folded her arms.

Richard shoved his hands into his coat pockets. "Merry Christmas," he said softly. He stepped toward her as if he might give her a hug, but thought better of it.

"Goodbye, Robert," she said.

"I'm Rich—" he started to say, then gave up. With a nod to Pop, he walked out.

Pop shook his head. "I feel sorry for you, Ethel."

"Keep your pity to yourself," she said, turning on him. "You don't know me."

"No, I don't. And it's just as well for the both of us," he said.

Pop noticed that Lillian had put on her coat again as if she was about to leave.

"You must be hot," Libby said and gently tugged at the shoulders.

Lillian pulled away. "I want to be ready when Ben gets here."

Libby guided her to a chair. "Lillian … maybe Ben won't make it this year." She eased them both down.

"He'll come," countered Lillian. "He said he would. In the letter."

"That's an old letter." Libby hesitated. "What if he doesn't make it for some reason? You don't want to spend the whole night waiting for him, do you?"

Lillian looked resolute. "He'll come."

Libby sighed, then stood up. "Suit yourself."

Lillian reached up and took hold of Libby's hand. "I don't want to be alone anymore, Libby. I don't want to be alone at Christmas."

"You're not alone, Lillian. I'm here. Henry, David, Veronica ... we're all here." Libby patted her hand. "We all love you, Lillian. You're not alone."

Libby went to a table with bowls of snacks. She began pushing the bowls into a line and arranging the paper plates and napkins.

Pop went over with an excuse to get a few pretzels.

"What's her story?" he asked Libby in a low voice.

"Lillian?" She consolidated two bowls of potato chips into one. "She's been carrying that letter for five years."

"Who is Ben?"

"Her son. He was a military contractor. He was killed in Afghanistan not long after that letter was written."

"She doesn't know?"

"She knows, but forgets. When we remind her, she is grief-stricken, as if she's hearing the news for the first time. So, sometimes, I try to work around it. I think disappointment is better than grief."

"Doesn't she have any other family?"

Libby shook her head. "We've tried to find them. Her husband died several years ago. Ben was her only child. He had a family— but there was some kind of falling out after he was killed."

Pop glanced over at Lillian. She was still sitting with her hands clasped on her lap. "So, every Christmas she sits and waits for someone who'll never come?"

Libby looked at him sadly. "That's how it is for a lot of people in here. They've been tucked away and forgotten."

"What about you?" Pop asked her.

She gave him a coy smile. "They have become my family."

Looking around the room, Pop thought, *So this is what happens after a lifetime of marriage and kids, work and play, happiness and hardship. You spend your days in a place like this, watching, wondering, waiting.*

They made a valiant attempt to play charades, but David's and Veronica's overall confusion usurped the experience. David got the rules completely mixed up, calling out titles for books when the category was movies, or singing a tune when the category was books. Veronica paid no heed to categories at all, turning every round into a chance to talk about the famous people she claimed to have known.

They eventually switched to simpler activities at different tables—cards and board games. Pop noticed that, as the night wore on, Lillian had taken off her coat and joined in a round of bingo. Pop also saw Miss Garcia slip in and take Lillian's suitcase away. He guessed that Lillian's expectation of a visiting son had faded away.

Throughout the evening, Ethel mocked and cajoled everyone—never a participant, always the heckler. Except the game of bingo. She was enthusiastic when it came to bingo.

As the night wound down, David began to sing "Auld Lang Syne." But few remembered all the lyrics and the song echoed away to nothing. All the same, David looked contented.

Miss Garcia appeared and reminded everyone about the gift exchange at eleven o'clock the next morning.

Veronica exclaimed, "Gifts! Oh, I love exchanging gifts!"

"Were we supposed to buy gifts?" David asked. "How was I supposed to buy gifts? I haven't left this place in three years."

Veronica hooked an arm through his and guided him to the door. "Oh, David, you're so senile!"

Pop joined Libby at the snack table. She was tidying up. "You know, they pay people to do that," he said. "Well, actually, *we* pay people to do that."

"I hate to leave them a big mess for Christmas Day," she said.

Pop watched as Henry crossed over to Ethel. "Shall I wheel you back to your room?" he asked.

"No. Just leave me be."

Henry backed away. "As you wish." He waved to the room. "Merry Christmas, everyone!"

"Ethel," Libby called out. "You should come back to my room for a cup of tea."

"No."

"You can't just sit here. They'll turn off the lights soon." Libby went to her. "I'll take you back to your room."

"I want to be left alone!" Ethel growled.

Libby looked at Pop and shrugged.

Pop helped Libby sweep the crumbs off the tables and tuck the chairs in. Ethel didn't look at them.

"Merry Christmas, Ethel," Libby said from the doorway.

"Christmas. Pooh," Ethel said.

Pop walked with Libby to the rooms. He patted his pockets to find his room key, then realized he'd left his jacket in the Sun Room. He told Libby and turned to go back.

Libby gave him a quick hug. "Merry Christmas," she said. "I'm glad you're here."

He smiled and retraced his steps to the Sun Room.

His jacket wasn't where he thought he'd put it. He must have left it in his room. From the corner of his eye, he saw Ethel at the coffee stand.

Her back was to him. He watched as she drained the last of the coffee into a cup. Then she lowered her head. Her shoulders began to shake. He heard her sob. She said in a thick voice, "That *stupid* boy."

Pop wanted to go to her. He hesitated. Then he took a step and his foot scraped loudly against the floor.

Ethel sat up; her shoulders erect. She stayed frozen where she was.

"Sorry," Pop said. "I thought I forgot my ... um ..."

"Goodnight," Ethel said without turning to him.

"Goodnight," Pop said and left her.

Pop went to his room and put on his best suit for the Midnight Mass. Then he put a few things into an overnight case. "Imagine that," he said to his favorite pajamas. "I have to pack to visit my own home."

Stepping back from the suitcase, he went through an inventory list in his mind. He didn't want to forget anything. It's not that the house was very far if he did—a few minutes—but he didn't want to ask anyone to bring him back. It would only reinforce what they already thought about his condition.

He was pretty sure he had what he needed. The checklist was fairly straightforward for the overnight stay. But he felt anxious as a question kept replaying in his mind. *Are you prepared?*

He looked down at his favorite pajamas and imagined them in a box, ready to go to the charity shop. No one else would want them. His favorite pajamas might be worn by a complete stranger in a year's time, maybe a few months. How could he know?

Are you prepared?

A cold panic gripped him. *Am I? Am I prepared?*

He had reached a stage of life where every large and small thing—Midnight Mass, a Christmas dinner, opening presents, a simple hello or a casual goodbye—could be the last thing.

Am I prepared for the last things? Pop wondered. He slumped down onto his bed. *I've had my whole life to get ready for this inevitable time. And I'm not sure I'm ready.*

PART THREE

THE SUN ROOM

Chapter 7

Pop's life at the Faded Flower had taken on a reassuring routine. There was security in knowing what to expect from day to day, hour to hour. He began to realize that he had entire portions of a day when he did not think about much. The latest news programs, a movie he had watched, some TV show he'd found shocking—these were distractions from any real thinking, something to make conversation about during meal times or in the Sun Room.

Other days, he thought too much. He mused about his future and wondered when the shades would be drawn in his mind. He considered the past and wondered how much he would remember of it.

Would he become the guy who could talk about the distant past while forgetting what had happened only yesterday? Then he wondered how long he would be able to wonder.

Would he have the self-awareness to know what was happening to him? Was it a mercy that he might not? Maybe the clues to the answers were already there. Hadn't he fought Minnie and Michael tooth-and-nail about his condition? Likely, he would do the same again, out of pride or fear or both.

One thing he noticed: his prayers had changed. He did more of them, with greater intention, as if preparing himself for the trouble to come. It was like storing ammunition for an impending battle. His prayers might be all that were left after he'd lost everything else.

When his wife died very suddenly a few years ago, Pop thought of death as an aberration. It wasn't something that was supposed to happen to those we love, but it might happen because the body we live in could have a weird shift—like a heart attack or a disease, or the world might have a weird glitch—like a car accident or a natural disaster. Otherwise, death was something that happened far off on the distant horizon of time.

Pop's condition changed all of that. Death was ever-present, a ticking stopwatch with missing hands.

How are we supposed to respond to death? Should we embrace it, like St. Francis did when he called her "Sister Death"? Is it a natural end to a natural life? If so, then why do we, as rational beings, resist it at the very core of our beings? And, for those who don't resist, why do we consider them depressed or suicidal? Shouldn't death be a horror to us, waylaid and fought at every turn?

Those questions were on his mind at that very moment as he sat in the Sun Room in his usual chair. He was looking out at a beautiful spring day. David sat in the chair next to him.

For Pop, David had become a kind of "Ghost of Christmas Yet to Come"—the person Pop could become in no time at all. The wiring in David's brain seemed to have come loose, causing their conversations to ricochet around with very little coherency. Pop found it was easiest to play the straight man in the comedy of old age.

Today, David was chatting about a brother who had died in a war.

"Which war?" Pop asked.

"The one where people were trying to kill each other."

"Oh. I remember that one."

"I was in seminary then," David said. "Until they carted me off to Fort Dix to be an assistant chaplain."

"You were a clergyman?"

David nodded. "Baptist. Back when it meant something."

"Like what?"

"Oh, you know. We took stands on all the important things, like drinking and smoking and dancing.

"The important things."

"And marriage," David added. "'Till death do us part' and all those other Bible verses. I don't understand these men who get married over and over. Except Brother Bennett."

"Never heard of him," Pop said.

"No reason you should," said David. "He was a deacon in my first church. Ninety-seven years old and he had been married seven times. Three of those were after he had turned eighty."

"He must have had a lot of stamina," Pop said.

"He did. A full head of hair. All of his original teeth. Impressive," David said. "He kept outliving them all. But his wives were good Baptist women, so it didn't seem like he was married more than the once."

Pop said, "You make them sound like interchangeable parts."

David gave a slight shrug. "They sang in the choir. Though his last wife—what was her name?—she was a strange one. She said she was against organized religion."

"I've never heard of a disorganized religion."

"She said the church wasn't bricks and mortar."

"What did she have against bricks and mortar?" Pop asked.

"Some loose ideas. Nothing concrete."

Pop looked at David and wondered if that was an intentional joke. "Did she have anything against wood?"

"The subject never came up," said David. "Though I think she buried Brother Bennett in a wooden coffin. So, she must have been all right with it for a few purposes."

"I'm glad. Plastic coffins don't work very well."

David paused for a moment, then said, "I was pastor of a little Baptist church in southwest Pennsylvania. That was back in the sixties."

"Yours or someone else's?"

"The *nineteen sixties*."

"That was a messy time," Pop said.

"You're telling me." David gave the room a quick glance. He lowered his voice and said, "I had a Ladies Auxiliary that nearly wrecked the church. Three of the women started wearing slacks to the services. One went *braless*, just to make a point."

"I meant, it was a messy time for the nation," Pop explained.

"Oh, in southwest Pennsylvania, we didn't worry much about the nation. Not when we had women wearing slacks to church." David glanced around again. "Women don't know what they do to men. By wearing slacks."

"Ah."

"They distract from the worship," David said.

"Hmm."

"Leaves nothing to the imagination."

"Oh."

"Robs men of their distinction."

"Ah."

"Robs men of their authority."

"Robs men of their wardrobe," Pop concluded.

David shook his head. "If women were intended to wear slacks, they would have been born men."

"Some wanted to be," Pop said. "I once knew a woman who said that fashion and marriage were a conspiracy by the Male Establishment to oppress women."

"A feminist."

"She said we should make love, not war."

"A pacifist."

"She believed in free love."

"An economist."

Pop did a double take. "What?"

"You said '*free* love.' It was the first word that came to my mind." David folded his arms. "The world was a mess. It still is. I did a whole series of sermons about it. Or maybe it was a letter to the newspaper."

"About what?"

"Life. Death. The futility of it all without Christ."

Pop chuckled. "I know a lot of futile Christians."

David sighed. "I don't understand why people these days want to choose death. We don't choose death. Death chooses us."

So true, Pop thought.

"I honestly can't think of what people are thinking when they think the things they're thinking," David lamented.

Pop agreed.

And then the chimes rang for lunch.

CHAPTER 8

THERE WAS a crisis in the Sun Room just after Easter. The ancient cassette player that sat on a side table was empty. Veronica had looked in the slot several times, then behind the player, then next to the player, but couldn't find what she was looking for.

"Where's my tape?" she asked everyone present.

Pop looked up from his place in his usual chair. David was next to him, looking particularly vacant. Ethel sat in her wheelchair in front of a television that wasn't on. Henry and Maggie were playing a card game at one of the tables.

"I left it here. I know I did," Veronica said. Since Pop was the only one looking her way, she zeroed in on him. "How long have you been here?" she asked.

"Oh, since shortly after I arrived," Pop said, borrowing something he'd heard David say.

"Have you seen my tape?" she asked.

"Which tape are you talking about?" Maggie asked as she played a card.

Veronica looked panicked. "The tape that has been in this player for months. The one with me singing. I play it every day. It's gone."

"Maybe it self-destructed," David said.

"Self-*what*?"

"Destructed," David said. "Like they used to do on that television show. You remember: 'This tape will self-destruct in thirty seconds.'"

"Are you saying my tape self-destructed?" Veronica asked, bewildered. "Why would it do that?"

"Suicide," Ethel said. "It couldn't stand to hear you singing again."

"Don't be unkind," Maggie said to Ethel.

Veronica looked wounded. "You're saying my tape committed suicide because of my singing?"

Ethel shrugged. "Why not? Your singing killed our houseplant."

Veronica gasped. "It did not!"

"It certainly did," said Ethel. "Miss Garcia had a healthy houseplant right next to the player and it died from listening to your tape."

Pop slowly shook his head. He had hoped that the regular visits from her grandson would have tempered Ethel's hurtfulness.

"Ethel, don't torture the poor girl," Henry said. "Where is her tape?"

Ethel looked indignant. "Are you saying that I took it? Is that what you're saying? You think I stole the tape?"

"I'm only asking everyone about it," Veronica said.

Libby came in with a puzzled look on her face. She held up a plastic bag. Inside was a cassette tape. But there was something wrong with its appearance. "I just found this in the trash next to the dining room."

Henry asked, "Why were you going through the trash?"

"Old habits die hard," Ethel said.

"I wasn't going *through* it. I was throwing something away and saw this on the top. Veronica, I think it's your tape."

Veronica rushed to her and took the bag. She held it up and winced, "Is that *asparagus*?"

"And applesauce," Libby said. "I'm sorry. The tape was covered with lunch. I wiped off what I could and put it in the bag."

"Why was it in the trash?" Veronica asked.

"Suicide," Ethel said.

"*Ethel*," Henry warned.

"This is terrible." Veronica waved a hand in front of her face. "I'm feeling faint. Oh, please, let me sit down."

With surprising agility, Henry grabbed a chair for her. She slumped down, clutching the sandwich bag of her tape to her breast.

She said, "My heart is racing."

"I'd be surprised if anything is racing in our bodies," Henry said.

"Strolling, then," Pop offered.

"Veronica—" Libby began, but Veronica was lost in her dramatic scene.

"I have a history of blood clots," Veronica announced. "If I feel too stressful, I could die of a blood clot. Right now, my whole body feels like a giant blood clot."

"Blood clots don't have legs," Ethel said.

"I might die today of a blood clot in my broken heart," Veronica said. "Why would someone throw a tape of my singing into the trash?"

"A shredder would have been better," Ethel said.

"I thought we cared about each other," Veronica said. "I thought we were family."

Libby went to Veronica and put a hand on her arm. "Veronica," she said softly. "I think *you* threw the tape away."

"What?"

"Don't you remember? You took the tape out of the machine earlier. You said you wanted to play it in your room. But you went to lunch first. I saw the tape sitting next to your plate. You had asparagus and applesauce with your sandwich. You picked it all up and went to the trash ..." Libby's voice faded.

Veronica lowered her head. "It was me? How could I forget such a thing?" she asked. An expression of complete helplessness crossed her face.

Pop looked away. Just yesterday, he was ready to accuse an orderly of stealing medicine from the cabinet in his room. He was in a full-blown rage over it. Then Michael pointed out that he'd left the medicine sitting on the windowsill near his bed.

"What's wrong with me?" Veronica asked.

The same thing that's wrong with all of us, Pop thought. *We're marching slowly to the end.*

CHAPTER 9

I T WAS AN overcast day early in the summer. Pop had awakened in a dark mood. Why? He didn't know. His mind went into an odd loop—recycling his hurt and anger over being told he could not teach at the church anymore. Though it had happened months ago, the moment came to him as a fresh wound. He had dedicated himself to teaching at the church for years and years.

David walked into the Sun Room, interrupting Pop's thoughts. David had been a Baptist pastor for years. Pop didn't know what the circumstances were behind David's retirement. He hadn't asked, since David's "on days" and "off days" were unpredictable. Today, there was a look in David's eyes that told Pop he was having an "on day."

"What becomes of a teacher who can't be a teacher anymore?" he asked David.

"Did my teaching reach an expiration date that nobody told me about?" Pop asked, after explaining about being asked to give up his classes.

David looked at him for a moment. "I felt like a man who had been evicted," he said. "Suddenly the leadership of the church decided that I should go. It was time to leave. And I was gone. Now here I am."

"Here *we* are," Pop said.

David's gaze went to the large window. "I think it's going to rain today."

"Why are we here?" Pop asked. "I'm asking you sincerely. Tell me why God has put us here?"

David sighed. "I know what I *could* say."

"What could you say?" Pop asked.

David lifted his hands from his lap. He intertwined his arthritic fingers as if he was about to pray. Pop wondered if this was the posture David took when he once counseled people in his office.

"I could tell you that God's ways are not our ways," David said. His voice sounded younger somehow. "There's a reason for this that we don't understand yet. I could quote the Apostle Paul and say that 'all things work together for the good of those who love God and are called according to his purpose.' I could say that God may use this suffering in your life in a way you don't see right now. I could add that the comfort that God gives to you now may well prove to be a comfort you give to others in the future. And I could finish by saying that you must yield to God, without bitterness, and he will give you grace in your time of need."

Pop was stunned. He wondered from what deep treasure David had drawn that answer. "Do you believe everything you just said?"

"Yes. But ..."

"But what?"

"I wouldn't really say all those things to you."

"Why not?"

"Because," he said slowly, "while I believe what I said, I don't believe you want to hear it."

"What do I want to hear?"

"What you want to hear is that I don't know why we're here. You want me to say that I don't know why we grow old and lose our ability to do things, or to think."

"Is that what I want?"

David nodded. "It's hard to grasp what God is doing. And any explanation sounds trite and meaningless."

"True."

"But I look at the Bible and I read the story in the Gospels of the man who was born blind and how Jesus spat in the dirt and wiped the mud on his eyes—and the man was healed. Why did that happen? Jesus said it happened for the glory of God."

Pop remembered the story. "That is what Jesus said."

"The man was blind from birth. But we don't know how long he was blind before Jesus healed him. And yet Jesus said that the reason for the man's blindness was to glorify God." David's eyes went up to the top of the window. A few drops of rain touched the glass and began to slide down. "Do you think the man railed at God for making him blind, or did he praise God for healing him?"

"The healing."

"That's right." David slowly nodded. "I think we've come to believe that God is here to make us happy. Few of us want to believe that we can glorify God in our suffering."

"But God can heal us."

"In his good time, if he wills it."

"That's too easy. Does God heal or doesn't he?"

"He can."

"So, he could heal any one of us now," Pop said. "You were a pastor. You could pray for me to be healed and he would do it. Go on. Pray. Or are you afraid?"

"I'm not afraid. But there's one thing I learned after I stopped being a pastor: don't be presumptuous. It's not a good idea to ask God for a miracle right at this minute."

Pop could feel a rage burning through him. "What's the point of a miracle if it doesn't happen when you pray for it? Is it so wrong to ask him *why*? Is it so wrong to say that I don't understand why I long for his touch but don't feel it, to long for a *whisper* and not hear a word, to expect the miracles he wrote an *entire book* about and not experience a single one?"

"What else is there? What do we know about such things? What do we *really* know? We're amateurs. Little children. Maybe that's why God makes us like little children at the end of it all. So, the only thing we have is faith."

Pop's anger washed over his eyes, like the raindrops on the glass, and obscured his vision.

David reached over and took Pop's hand. He looked earnestly into Pop's eyes. "There's a van. For trips to the store and doctor's appointments. I know where they keep the keys. We could take the van and drive anywhere we want. Tour the mountains. Drive to Mexico."

"I've never been to Mexico." Pop took a deep breath, willing his anger to dissipate. "I read the Spanish culture has a deep regard for old people. They respect them. How they do it with those goofy hats is another question."

"Sombreros."

"Isn't that an afternoon nap?" Pop asked.

"I could use one of those now," said David.

Pop thought about it. "Mexico is very flat. Perfect for old people to get around."

"How do you know?"

"It looks flat on the map," Pop said. "But I heard the water there upsets the stomach. I don't want to die of flatulence in a foreign country. Besides, my wife is buried here."

"We could steal the van and go to town for ice cream," David said. "We'll need umbrellas, though."

"*Or* we could avoid getting wet and have some of the ice cream they serve here," Pop suggested.

That's what they decided to do.

Pop would later recall that it was the last coherent conversation he ever had with David.

PART FOUR

THE LAST THINGS

Chapter 10

G OD, WHAT *are you doing to me?*
    That's the question Michael had been asking for the past year. Colleen called it his refrain.

Apart from asking God that question, Michael wasn't sure he'd be talking to God at all. He felt guilty about that—especially since he was still a regular churchgoer. He didn't know what to do with his feelings of anger. Was it right to take it out on God? He suspected it wasn't, and tried to compensate by praying longer, or reading devotional pieces his wife had around the house. Often, he felt just as angry as he did when he started. More so, sometimes.

"Many of the Psalms were written by men who were angry with God," Father Cliff Montgomery reminded Michael during Confession one day. "And I think God is big enough to endure your anger—and your silence. The fact that you're angry with God means that, at the very least, you haven't stopped believing in him."

Michael thought about it after he left the confessional and decided that the main reason he had stopped talking to God was

173

because God had stopped talking to him. Their communication shut down on the day he'd lost his job and began to lose his father.

"A little higher, Michael," Father Cliff said, bringing him back to the present.

Michael was standing on a ladder in the Sun Room with a mouth full of thumbtacks, pressing the end of a banner against the wall. It said "Happy Birthday!" in bright purple sparkly letters. Stars burst all around it. Michael mumbled through his clenched lips, "Higher? Are you sure?"

Father Cliff assured him he was sure.

Michael lifted the banner higher. "How's that?" he asked.

Father Cliff gave him a thumbs-up.

Climbing down from the ladder, Michael took a few steps back to see the banner for himself. The lettering had been hand-printed by a resident named Libby Caldwell. "No computer printouts for Pop," she said when Michael had the audacity to suggest the idea. "I'll take care of it." And she did.

The coloring and starbursts around the letters had been painted by some of the Faded Flower's other residents. They liked Pop and were happy to contribute to his birthday party.

"It's hanging low on the left," Michael said to Father Cliff.

"Really? I think it's perfectly fine," Father Cliff said genially. "Don't you trust me?"

"Not when it comes to the positioning of great art," Michael said. "I've seen what you've done at the rectory."

Father Cliff chuckled. Having Father Cliff at the Faded Flower was a refreshing change from the wrinkles, false teeth, and bedpans that Michael saw while working as a part-time handyman there.

"Aren't you afraid your father will see the banner before his party?" Father Cliff asked.

"He's leaving his room less and less these days," Michael said. Pop's condition had degenerated in the ten months since they'd brought him to the Faded Flower. He had good days and bad days, but never an improvement. Michael saw only the slow descent into deep shadows he didn't understand. Sometimes his father spoke of distant memories in the present tense. It was a characteristic of many of the residents there. It could be a look someone would see in his own eyes in another twenty years.

"I wonder if he's gotten worse because of the move," Michael said.

"How can you know?" Father Cliff asked. "Maybe you moved him just in the nick of time. There's no telling what harm he'd have done to himself if you left him at home."

Michael wanted to believe him. "You and my wife are cut from the same cloth," he said.

"How so?"

"She's always so upbeat and optimistic about everything," Michael said. "When I couldn't find a job, she said it was a blessing in disguise. 'Must be a really good disguise,' I said. When we had to sell our own house in order to make ends meet, she said she wouldn't miss the place. She seemed *happy* to move into a smaller house here. She said it was like coming home again, even though this was never really her home."

"Has she been wrong?" Father Cliff asked.

Michael had to think about the question. "She said this whole situation was God's way of bringing me closer to my father, even though my father is drifting away from me."

Father Cliff busied himself with the decorations, allowing Michael to chatter on.

"Now that I think about it, the only change in her life that *didn't* get a positive response was when Ethan moved out." Michael frowned, remembering the day. "She showed us a brave face when he packed up his old Subaru and pulled out of the driveway. But I know she'd shed a lot of quiet tears. She prayed like I'd never seen before."

"Has Ethan discovered America?" Father Cliff asked. "Wasn't that his plan?"

"I told him that he was five hundred years too late," Michael said. "Madison said he was being so *sixties*. She bought him a psychedelic headband and love beads as a going-away present. I can't imagine where she found them. And I bought him a small model of a chopper motorcycle."

"A chopper?"

"Like the one Dennis Hopper rode in *Easy Rider*. Ethan put it on his dashboard."

"Who is Dennis Hopper?" Father Cliff asked.

"Never mind," Michael said.

Ethan's last letter was postmarked from Albuquerque, New Mexico. He was working as a waiter at night and spending his days designing websites for local companies. Michael still felt stung that Ethan had gone off on what Michael felt was a self-indulgent excursion rather than focus on meaningful steps toward a proper future. He'd made it clear that none of the money from the college fund would go to his trip. Though, Michael suspected that Colleen was still funneling money to their son in other ways.

Michael also felt bothered that his son wasn't around for this difficult period of life. "But the boy had to do what he had to do," Pop once said, "and suffer the consequences along with his decision."

Ed Powell, a resident with a permanent stoop, entered the Sun Room. He held up the morning newspaper. "Helen Altman passed away from bone cancer," he announced. "She is survived by her husband, Joseph, and daughters JoAnne M. and Carol and Mary, a son, Glen A. Four brothers and sisters."

"Be quiet!" Barry Fitzgibbons shouted from a chair in front of the television.

Ed Powell read even louder, "Rosary will be held Sunday, October 17th at the Hudson Brothers Funeral Home."

The Hudson Brothers, Michael thought. He remembered Billy and Jamie Hudson from elementary school. They were a couple of thugs who'd pestered him for his lunch money nearly every day. Leave it to them to find a future in no future—and still rob people in the process.

"John Keller passed away—"

"Quiet!" Emma Dickins said from a table where she was diligently knitting something orange and green.

"Quiet yourself!" Mr. Powell shouted back and then continued, "John Keller passed away from natural causes—"

"What does 'natural causes' mean?" Michael asked Mr. Powell, hoping to distract him.

Mr. Powell looked startled by the question.

Father Cliff smiled. "I think it means nothing artificial with no preservatives?"

Confused by their exchange, Mr. Powell scowled at Michael and Father Cliff, then harrumphed and dropped into one of the deck chairs, muttering as he continued to read to himself.

Libby was at Michael's side. "It looks wonderful," she said about the banner. Her eyes then darted around the room and Michael knew she was considering what other arrangements to make for Pop's birthday. She seemed to have a great affection for Pop and wanted everything to be perfect. Not that Pop would notice.

More than once Michael wondered what Libby was doing at the Faded Flower. She was a strong, levelheaded, and compassionate woman who'd been in upper management at a company in Greeley for years. She certainly didn't seem to need assistance. But Michael had heard that she'd forfeited ever having a family for her career and would have lived alone if she hadn't come there. She was now like an Angel of Energy and did all she could to keep everyone involved and active. Some of the folks didn't always appreciate her enthusiasm. Michael had heard the curmudgeony Ethel sarcastically called her a *One-Woman Glee Club* on more than one occasion.

"Ah! I nearly forgot," Libby proclaimed and raced out of the room.

"Thank you for your help, Father Cliff," Michael said and folded up the ladder. He carried it across to a utility closet on the far side of the room, passing Don and Bob—two friends who bickered like an old married couple—as he went. At the moment, Bob was showing off his new typewriter to Don. It was an antique Underwood.

"But where did you get it?" Don was asking impatiently, as if he'd asked the question before and never got an answer.

"Oh. This was a present from my son-in-law. So I could write," Bob replied as he started to hunt-and-peck his way around the keyboard.

Don wasn't impressed. "In an age where portable computers can fit in your shirt pocket and do a heart massage on you while you catch a bus, your son-in-law bought you an old *typewriter*?"

"They can not!" Bob protested.

"Sure they can. I read about it in a magazine just the other day."

"A portable computer that can fit in your shirt pocket?"

"Uh huh." Don tapped the pocket over his chest. "Right there. Snug as a bug in a rug."

"And do a heart massage on you."

"Well ... why not?" Don asked.

"How does it penetrate the skin?"

"What?"

"To do a heart massage, it would have to penetrate the skin. That would make you bleed, which would ruin your shirt. And it would have to somehow get past your rib cage to get to your heart to give it a massage. That would be painful. Too painful to run with. I broke a rib once, so I know about these things." Bob sounded exasperated.

"What are you saying?" Don asked.

"I'm *saying* that there's no way you could be running to catch a bus while all these things are going on under your shirt."

Don rolled his eyes. "I'm only telling you what I read in a magazine."

"It's not possible." Bob waved at Father Cliff. "Young man! Tell him it's not possible."

The last thing Father Cliff wanted to do was get in the middle of one of their arguments. He said, "I think anything is possible these days."

"There," Don said.

"It's not possible," Bob maintained.

Michael chuckled as he put the ladder in the closet. Father Cliff peeked in and said, "I'm going to say a quick hello to your father"—and left.

Michael locked the closest again and headed toward the door. Veronica Talbot was there, her arms spread dramatically across the doorframe. She wore a loose-fitting robe made up of a dull yellow pattern of flowers. She had once been an actress and, even now, reminded him of Norma Desmond arriving for her close-up in *Sunset Boulevard*. He suspected that was her intention.

"Hello, *darling*," Veronica said a cough-syrup voice.

"Hello, Mrs. Talbot," Michael replied politely, hoping to get past her without a long exchange.

"Call me Veronica. *Please*. It's what all my friends do."

Michael smiled. They'd had this same conversation nearly every day since he went to work for the Faded Flower. "Yes, ma'am." But Michael wouldn't call her Veronica. Especially since he took her up on the offer once and she immediately shouted, "How dare you call me by my first name! I am Mrs. Talbot to the *help*!"

"I remember Kirk Douglas once said to me ...," she started to say.

Michael feigned something catching his attention just over her shoulder. He excused himself and left. He wasn't interested in another story about Kirk Douglas. Or the *same* story about Kirk Douglas.

As Michael walked down the hall, he thought again about the year since Pop's last birthday—that awful, terrible birthday—and the twists and turns of his life. There were days when he was convinced he'd wake up in his own bed, back in his old house in Denver. He'd get up and go to work at the Bradlow Company and life would be what it once was, the nightmare over. But then there was always a reminder that brought him back to the present like a cold, wet slap in the face. Sometimes it was the feel of the overalls against his legs rather than the lighter brush of suit trousers. Sometimes it was the sound of a metal walker clacking its way down the hall. Sometimes it was the smell of cleaning chemicals.

So, this is what it comes down to, he often thought. Like so many of the old folks around the Faded Flower, he'd been stripped of almost everything he once held dear. Even his memories of his father were being taken away from him. Just like the memories of his mother. When he thought of her now, all that came to mind was her lying in the coffin, a poor waxen representation of the woman he knew. And he recognized that, in the future, memories of his father would be dominated by these last days at the Faded Flower.

"Think of the good things, Michael. *Fight* to think of the good things. *Remember*," Colleen once pleaded with him.

Yes, the good things. Like the day Pop had bought him a secondhand bike and then tried to teach him to ride. He wrecked three or four times and then realized he was better off without his father's help. Years later he learned that his dad didn't know how to ride a bike.

There was the time he fell backward off the porch swing—he'd been standing on the seat, though he'd been told a hundred times not to. Pop had to carry him a mile to the doctor because the car wouldn't start, and the ambulance was on another call. He got blood all over his dad's new shirt.

The memories came fast and furious. But then, like a rubber band snapping into place, he was brought back to the Faded Flower.

———————————◆———————————

What are you doing to me, God?

He'd been struggling with this question for a year now and didn't see the point. *God's not giving me a clue. He keeps throwing changes at me with no instruction manual for dealing with them.*

"Oh, get over it, Michael," Aunt Minnie once said when she'd grown tired of his complaining. "So, the Lord took away all your security blankets. Is that such a bad thing?"

He didn't give her an answer. That was the thing about self-pity, he supposed. It closed all the doors and windows to the fresh air of a better perspective. Privately he had to admit that things hadn't been as bad as they could have been. He still had Colleen and Madison, a place to live, a job (of sorts), and his health. He could concede that much with a certain amount of gratitude. *I'm no Job; I know that*, he admitted. *But if God is responsible for taking everything else away from me, would it be asking too much to find out the reason?*

Sometimes he worried that he had too much time on his hands to think. His job gave him a lot of solitary time while he fixed a bed or adjusted a loose cupboard door or cleared leaves from the gutters. It was an old building with a lot of repair needs. He supposed that was why he kept coming back to his refrain: *What are you doing to me, God?*

He'd posed that question to Father Cliff. The priest only shrugged. "You're on a pretty wild spiritual journey and it wouldn't be right for me to guess at God's intentions."

One day he got annoyed and said, "You're a priest, for crying out loud. If *you* can't guess, then who can?"

He smiled. "A better priest?"

———————————◆———————————

It was Deacon Chuck Crosby from St. Clare's who'd said, "We all have to make a choice about what we believe."

"What choice?" Michael asked.

"You can believe that God doesn't exist. Or you can believe he exists but doesn't care about your problems. Or, worse, you can believe he exists and is maliciously causing your problems for his own warped pleasure. Or you can believe he exists and loves you and your problems are somehow a mysterious extension of that love."

"Quite a selection," said Michael.

"And we don't make the choice one day and live with that choice for the rest of our lives."

"We don't?"

With a shake of his bald head, Deacon Chuck said, "Most of us are choosing every day, depending on what life throws at us."

Was that perspective helpful? Michael wasn't sure. But he thought about it a lot.

He wasn't blind to the different ways God had repeatedly put him in the path of church people. Shortly after moving back to Hope Springs, he found himself helping out with odds and ends at the church. A quick favor here and a little job there. Before he realized what was happening, he had gone to Confession and was attending Mass regularly with Colleen and Madison again.

Colleen occasionally teased him about going, since he still insisted he was not speaking to God. He told her it was merely an excuse to wear a suit and tie again, though few people wore suits or ties to church anymore.

"You and our Lord are in cahoots and you don't even realize it," Colleen said.

Michael slipped into Pop's room after escaping from Madam Movie Queen Veronica. He wasn't terribly surprised to see the wrapper of a 3 Musketeers candy bar sitting on the end table next to Pop's favorite chair. That was sure evidence that Father Cliff had been there, as promised. The priest always smuggled one in. Until Father Cliff came along, Michael had no idea his father had such a weakness for chocolate. The 3 Musketeers bars in particular.

Michael touched the brown-and-green wingback chair that sat incongruously in the room. It was one of the few reminders his father had of his old home. Though, Pop rarely sat in it now. Lately he'd been using a wheelchair. It wasn't that he couldn't walk anymore, but he seemed to have lost interest in the activity after he'd fallen down a couple of months ago. That's when they moved him from the self-service apartment in the one wing and into an apartment in the "assisted living" wing.

"Dad?" Michael called out.

Pop's room, by most standards, was pretty comfy. If the bed wasn't so clearly hospital-like, the room might have looked like any one-bedroom apartment. It had a small living area with a television, a bedroom area, and a kitchenette with a sink, a small fridge, and even a dishwasher. This particular unit didn't have a stove—a safety precaution against forgotten lit burners.

One of the differences from the non-assisted units was the signage. Signs hung on the drawers and doors reminding Pop of what was inside: "Plates" and "Food" and "Utensils." Otherwise, Pop couldn't remember where to look for things. There were also French doors that led out to a patio, though they were kept locked so that Pop wouldn't go wandering without an escort.

Right now, the doors were open. Cool autumn air slipped in, and Michael could see the rear grounds of the estate beyond. The trees had long shed their leaves, but the grass was still mostly green.

This is nothing to complain about, Michael thought every time he went into Pop's apartment. But he also acknowledged that they paid dearly for it, using the money from his dad's pension, the proceeds from the sale of the Denver house, some cashed-in life insurance, and Michael's own retirement savings.

All the same, Pop liked to complain about the space.

"Like father, like son," Madison once quipped.

A toilet flush drew Michael's attention to the bathroom door. He felt a twinge of worry. If Pop was in the bathroom, then who had opened the patio doors?

The answer came when Aunt Minnie walked in from the patio carrying a large plastic bag.

She smiled and said, "Oh, hello, Michael. I thought I'd slip out while your father was in the *you know*."

He smiled back, amused by her generation's inability to use words like *toilet* because they were indiscreet. He kissed her on the cheek and said, "I didn't know you were here."

"It's his birthday, isn't it?"

"But the party isn't until later."

"I wanted to wish him a happy birthday before the party overwhelmed him."

Michael hooked a thumb toward the bathroom. "How is he today? I haven't had a chance to see him until now."

"I think he may have a fever," Aunt Minnie said, concerned. Michael saw afresh how much she had aged since Pop had been admitted to the Faded Flower. There were new lines around her eyes and mouth. Or maybe they weren't new. Maybe they were just deeper than they were before.

"I'll tell Dr. Janssen," Michael promised.

The bathroom door opened and Pop, in the wheelchair, pushed himself out into the room. He saw Aunt Minnie and Michael talking and frowned. "What are you saying over there?"

"Nothing, Dad," Michael replied.

"You're saying something," he said, his tone a warning. In the last month or so he'd become paranoid that people were talking about him.

"I was telling Michael that I think you have a fever," Aunt Minnie explained. "Your forehead is hot."

"Of course my forehead is hot. It's hot in here. If you want cold, then check my feet," Pop said. He picked up his hat from a side table. It was the same hat he'd found in the attic a year ago.

Michael held up the 3 Musketeers bar wrapper. "Father Cliff was here," he said, pretending not to know that the priest was in the building.

Pop wheeled closer. "Yes, he was. I'll wager neither of you thought to bring me a candy bar," he said.

"Did you have a nice visit with him?" Aunt Minnie asked.

"I don't like that boy. Not one bit."

"Yes, you do," Aunt Minnie reminded him.

"He keeps threatening to let the air out of my tires," Pop said, tapping the wheels on his chair.

Aunt Minnie *tsked* at Pop. "He's teasing you."

"He stole my watch, too," Pop said.

"No, he didn't," Michael explained for the umpteenth time. "I took it to the jeweler's to be fixed. Remember?"

"What's in the bag?" Pop asked Aunt Minnie.

Aunt Minnie smiled coyly. "A few things."

"Toilet paper? Did you bring toilet paper?" he asked. "I hate the toilet paper they give us here. It's made by a sandpaper company in Phoenix."

"It isn't, but I brought you some anyway." Aunt Minnie took out a package of toilet paper and held it up like a trophy. "I got you a new toothbrush, too," she said as if offering him a new toy.

"A new toothbrush?"

"You said the other one made your gums bleed. This one will work if you use the end with the *brush*." Aunt Minnie handed the toilet paper and toothbrush to him.

Pop nodded appreciatively. "Did you have a good drive here? The roads were okay?"

"They were fine."

"It rained all morning, you know. I was afraid the roads would be wet."

It hadn't rained at all that morning and Michael nearly said so. But then thought there was no point.

Aunt Minnie patted him on the shoulder. "Not a thing to worry about. The roads were dry as a bone." She then took a wrapped present out of the bag and handed it to him. "Here. Happy birthday, James." She took the hat from his head and kissed him on the forehead. Then she dropped the hat back in place. She mouthed the word *fever* to Michael.

Pop looked at the present with undisguised worry. "What's this?"

"Open it."

Pop studied it for a moment and then put it aside. "I'll wait."

"I'm sorry," Aunt Minnie said. "I'll open it for you."

Before Pop could answer, Aunt Minnie took the present and carefully undid the ribbon. She then opened the wrapping to show the box inside. "Here you go."

Pop was able to manage the box.

"It's a large-print edition of the Bible," Aunt Minnie said, just in case.

"Oh. How nice," Pop said. "This is wonderful. Do I need this?"

"Yes. So you can read at night before you go to sleep."

Pop frowned. "Where's my old Bible?"

"You gave it to Ethan for his trip," Michael said. "The print was too small for you anyway. Remember? You gave it to him when you moved here."

"Oh. Yes. I moved." Pop looked at Aunt Minnie, his eyes filled with bewilderment. "I didn't like moving, did I, Minnie?"

"No, you didn't," she affirmed. "But you like it here now."

"Do I? Good," Pop said, his smile crooked. "Do they miss me at the Senior Citizens' Social?" he asked.

Aunt Minnie sat down on Pop's wingback chair. "Of course we do. Nobody could play charades like you."

"Or checkers."

"Nobody *wanted* to play checkers like you," Aunt Minnie said quickly.

Michael laughed.

"Have you been out for a stroll yet?" she asked.

"You mean a *ride*," Pop said. "No. But it'll be hard pushing through the snow."

"Let's try anyway." Aunt Minnie stood up and moved behind the wheelchair. She pushed Pop toward the patio doors.

Michael knew it wouldn't be much of a ride. Aunt Minnie would take Pop out onto the patio, then bring him in again.

"Minnie, why don't you move here to live? We could have a lot of fun," Michael heard Pop say.

"I can't now, James. I'm having the dining room repainted."

"Oh."

Aunt Minnie smiled at Michael just before they disappeared through the French doors.

Michael's phone vibrated in his pocket. He glanced down at the screen. Colleen was calling. He touched the button to accept the call.

"Is everything ready for the big surprise?" she asked.

Michael moved out of his dad's room. "I've been thinking about it," he said. "I'm not sure a surprise party is such a good idea."

"Why not?"

"I'm afraid he'll have a heart attack in front of everyone."

"That group won't notice," she said without missing a beat. Michael could almost hear her smile through the phone. "I have a couple of surprises for you."

"Surprises in our family are usually bad news," he said.

She was still smiling, he knew, as he heard her moving paper around. "There's a letter here from Cohen & Marx Publishing in Baltimore. It was forwarded from our old address."

"Cohen & Marx wrote to me?" Michael asked. Cohen & Marx was a small but influential publishing company that specialized in up-and-coming authors. He vaguely remembered applying there after he'd been let go from Bradlow. They had no openings for him then. "I'm surprised they mailed a letter. My résumé had my email and phone number."

"Do you want me to open it?"

"Sure, go ahead."

He could hear her slicing the letter open. "It's from ... Rory Zemeckis."

The name meant nothing to him.

Colleen gasped. "He wants you to contact him. They're revamping their editorial department and want you to interview."

"You're kidding." Michael's heart skipped a beat. *I'm wanted for a job interview?* He tried to remember who Rory Zemeckis was. Suddenly it clicked. He'd met Rory at a seminar a couple of years ago. They'd talked about editorial trends and the impact of technological changes on smaller businesses. It seemed to him then that they'd connected in a friendly, professional sort of way.

Colleen gasped again. "There's a handwritten note at the bottom."

"And?"

Colleen laughed.

"What's funny?"

His wife struggled to compose herself. "The note says, 'My sister Sally Quinten sends her regards.'"

"Sally Qu—?" Michael asked, and then the name registered. "*Spooky Sally?*"

Colleen laughed again.

Michael remembered well her vision that he would be living near his father again. And now, as then, he bristled. "She gives me the creeps."

"She may be giving you a job," Colleen said.

"Well, we'll see about that." The good news didn't seem as good anymore. He didn't like the feeling that Sally was manipulating things, even on behalf of God.

Colleen clearly knew what he was thinking and said, "She must have mentioned you to her brother. That's all. He wouldn't have written if he didn't think you were qualified for the job. You sent them a résumé, didn't you?"

"Yes." He had to shake off the bizarre feelings that Sally's name conjured up. Why should he care where the job opportunity came from? Why not be grateful? It was a new chance—a fresh beginning. "Please bring the letter when you come for the party," he said. He was about to say goodbye, but thought to ask, "Oh— and what's the other surprise?"

"I'll bring that when I come, too."

Toolbox in hand, Michael went to the lobby of the Faded Flower to adjust a few hinges on a cabinet for the coffee stand. He had built the cabinet himself, a proud accomplishment for such a small purpose. But some of the residents, while looking for creamer or sweeteners, used the doors as crutches. The hinges slowly came loose. As he worked, he realized he felt exhilarated by the letter from Cohen & Marx. *Somebody is interested in me again. I may be able to go back to work in a real office with real businesspeople. This could be a turning point.*

Just as quickly as the thought came, another feeling hit him: don't get your hopes up. In the days it took the letter to bounce from Denver to Hope Springs, the job might have already been filled. *I should get the phone number from Colleen and call Rory right away. Maybe my old professional instincts have completely dried up.*

He took out his phone to call his wife. He was about to punch the button for her number, but he hesitated. She would be at the Faded Flower soon enough. It could wait. And he had to think of what he'd say to Rory anyway. A question like, "So what have you been doing?" could throw him. "Handyman at a retirement center" wouldn't sound impressive.

After adjusting the hinges on the cabinet, he got up to leave. He looked around the lobby, which was once the front hall of the Grayson Mansion. A certain grandeur remained. It was easy to imagine the tuxedoed and bejeweled people entering for the parties held by oil baron Stephen Grayson. They would come in through the large front door, with its rose-shaped stained glass. The guests would have placed their calling cards on a silver tray held by a butler standing next to the gigantic round oak table (along with the gilded vase filled with the day's cuttings of flowers). Directly beyond the table, the guests would have admired the broad, red-carpeted stairs leading up to a landing where more stained glass adorned the windows. No doubt many of the guests wished they could ascend those stairs to see the many rooms on the second floor. But few of them would be allowed the privilege. Instead, they would be announced to the dark-paneled main drawing room off to the side, where they would admire the hand-carved hearth and crystal chandelier. *Oh, the glory of days gone by*, Michael thought.

Now, the wheelchair carrier lined one side of the stairs. A couple of residents complained that it had been acting up. So Michael hunched over the mechanism and opened the power box. With his limited experience, he couldn't see anything obvious. An electrician would have to be called.

He stood for a moment, tapping a screwdriver against his hand. He imagined himself back in an office, attending meetings, drinking coffee with his co-workers, writing proposals, talking on the phone to authors, shaking hands, and interpreting publishing trends. He sighed and looked down at his hands. They were shaking: adrenaline fueled by wishful thinking and a deep-seated insecurity. He'd been out of the game for a year. Was it possible to go back and find success?

He shrugged off the question. He would rise to the occasion and show everyone that he hadn't gone rusty. He'd show God.

Then the thought occurred to him that maybe this was God's answer to his prayer. Maybe God was finally going to come through for him.

Kneeling next to the toolbox, he put the screwdriver away and rubbed his temples. His head was beginning to hurt. Was this an answer to prayer? He had assumed his current situation was temporary, that whatever penance he had to pay for whatever sins he'd committed would eventually end. One way or another, he would go back to where he belonged. But now he had to wonder.

Where do I belong?

Colleen and Madison arrived carrying a couple of trays of goods they'd baked together at home. They were red-cheeked and excited, jabbering like two best friends.

"There's more in the car," Colleen said breathlessly to Michael after giving him a quick kiss. They headed down the hall for the Sun Room.

Michael stepped outside into the late afternoon mix of sun and clouds. He shivered at the cooling air. Where had the day gone? He hadn't realized it was getting so late.

The trunk lid of the car yawned at him. The floor was littered with trays of baked goods. He juggled two and turned back toward the Faded Flower. He paused. In the dusk, the mansion looked very cozy with its large ivy-covered stones. Dull yellow light burned in some of the windows. He saw figures moving. The hall lights, which were timed to turn on at that moment, highlighted the light green Victorian wallpaper. He saw Colleen and Madison enter the front hall again, returning for more trays. Madison was laughing and talking excitedly about something.

Madison, he thought. Since Pop's last birthday, she had moved gracefully into womanhood, without any of the angst or bad attitudes her old friends used to have. She gave every impression of liking Hope Springs. She seemed to like all the folks at the Faded Flower, showing none of the hesitancy to be around old people that young people often did. They treated her like a granddaughter. Even more surprising, Madison acted as if she enjoyed having Michael and Colleen around. His part-time schedule was flexible enough for them to sneak off to a matinee after she got out of school, or meet for lunch and have a picnic in the park. *I should be relishing these days*, Michael thought. *None of this would have happened with my old job.*

As his wife and daughter came outside, Michael wondered what the two of them thought about his potential job offer. Were they for it or against it? Colleen had betrayed nothing on the phone—not that he gave her the chance to say.

As she passed him, Colleen held up the letter and then tucked it into his overalls pocket. "You should get those trays inside before you drop them," she advised.

He realized he'd been standing there like a dolt, balancing the two trays. "So, what about it?" he asked Colleen, drawing her into the middle of his thoughts. "Is this a good thing?"

"Let's talk about it later. Right now, we have to get ready for Pop's party," she said.

"*Everybody's* coming," Madison exclaimed. "We invited everyone we could think of. Even Pop's old friends from church."

"It could be sensory overload for him," Michael cautioned.

In the Sun Room, Michael watched Madison arrange a large tray of cupcakes onto plates. Her face had lost its round babyness. Her body was changing its proportions. She didn't squeal and shout anymore. Now she spoke in the same level tones as her mother. The frantic pace she had kept in Denver was gone. She was still active at school and church, but she was more relaxed. He couldn't remember the last time she'd asked about getting a tattoo or a piercing. She embodied change. He wondered when people reached a stage where they resisted it.

"You like it here, don't you?" he asked, coming alongside her.

"The Faded Flower?"

"Hope Springs."

"Yes."

"What do you think of my possible job offer?" he asked her.

She hesitated—it was so slight Michael almost missed it—but he realized its significance. She was weighing her response. She was thinking about *him*. She didn't want to leave Hope Springs. But that wasn't what she said. She smiled at him. "I'll go if you want to go."

It was very brave of her. But he saw the thin line of worry crease her brow. Just like her mother.

He surveyed the trays and the room. "Where's the other surprise?" he asked.

"Ask Mom," Madison said.

Colleen was in the kitchenette next to the Sun Room. She was fiddling with the knobs for the burners on the stove.

"The other surprise?" Michael asked her.

"In Pop's room," she said nonchalantly.

They'd bought a present for his father, Michael guessed. Then he hoped that it wasn't too expensive. It wasn't that he worried about the money, but that an expensive present for Pop would be like giving a Mercedes Benz to a one-year-old.

Madison joined Colleen in the kitchenette. Michael felt he'd only get in the way if he hung around. He ventured back to Pop's room. The door was standing open. He peered in. Like before, no one was there. He stepped forward, looking around for the present. He didn't see anything obvious.

Suddenly a head peeked out of the bathroom, startling him. "Good heavens!" He nearly stumbled backward.

"Hi, Dad," Ethan said.

Michael hardly recognized his son. He was tanned and clean-shaven, with close-cut hair and an earring in his left ear. He wore a loose shirt but filled it out with broader shoulders and arms thick with muscles. He had on torn, stained jeans, and worn work boots. He looked healthier than Michael could have imagined.

Ethan smiled at Michael nervously.

Michael couldn't have explained to anyone the collision of feelings he was experiencing. Even as his heart leapt at the sight of his son, even as he wanted to grab him and pull him close for a hug, even as he believed he should speak affectionately, he did none of those things. "Is this someone I know?" he asked—a joke that sounded like a jab.

A shadow crossed Ethan's face.

"Wait," Michael continued. "Now I remember. You're the kid who gave up college to … what is it you do? Pump gas? No, that's not it. Sweep up after the horse races? No, that was last spring. Oh, I remember! You're in charge of the french fries at McDonald's. Have you mastered the art of deep fried, golden brown yet?"

"Close, but not quite," Ethan said with forced politeness. "Construction by day, computers by night."

"Calluses instead of a college degree," Michael said.

Ethan stiffened. "Dad, I'm not here to argue. I came to celebrate Pop's birthday."

"Thank you for that much," Michael said, regretting his tone but unable to change it. "Don't be surprised if he doesn't remember you, for as little as you've been around."

Ethan held up his hands in resignation. "No contest."

"Where is your grandfather?" Michael went to the French doors. They were closed. He looked out. It was ages ago that Aunt Minnie took Pop outside for a walk.

"I don't know," Ethan said.

"I'll check the hall," Michael said and started for the door.

"I figured out why you're so mad," Ethan said abruptly.

"Mad?" Michael asked. "What makes you think I'm mad?"

"It's not about college," Ethan said.

"It isn't?"

"No. You're mad because I diverged from your plans," Ethan said. "Do you realize you haven't once asked me if I'm happy? But I am, Dad. I like what I do. I work with my hands and my brain."

"Good," Michael said. "You're happy. I'm happy that you're happy, even though I think it's a waste."

Ethan folded his arms. "Then you must be especially mad about the twenty years you wasted at the Bradlow Company, right?"

Michael noticed a small tattoo on one of Ethan's arms. He hoped Madison wouldn't see it. "My time at Bradlow was not wasted," he said, trying to stay calm. "It fed you, it put a roof over your head, it put clothes on your back. How can you call my life's work wasted?"

"Is that what it was? Your life's work?" Ethan asked.

"I'm not going to stand here and be lectured by you," Michael said. "I lost my job. It wasn't my choice. You are making a choice." He was about to turn on his heels and walk out when Aunt Minnie wheeled Pop in from the hall.

"What's all the ruckus?" Pop asked loudly. "You're making enough noise to wake the dead."

"Oh, I hope not," Aunt Minnie said. "I've got relatives I don't want to see again." She winked at Michael.

Pop stretched his arms out to Ethan. "The prodigal has returned!"

Ethan hugged him. "Hi, Pop."

Pop gave him hard thumps on the back. "How have you been, boy?"

"Great. Things couldn't be better," Ethan said, with a sidelong glance at Michael.

"How's college?" Pop asked.

It was Michael's turn to give Ethan a sidelong glance.

Ethan knelt next to Pop's wheelchair. "I'm not in college, Pop. You know that."

"But you have to go to college," Pop said. "That's where I met your grandmother."

Aunt Minnie rolled her eyes. "Here we go."

"We met in the library and she was ..." Pop paused, his shaggy eyebrows knitted together over his eyes. "I was on the steps. I sang to her on the steps with a guitar. A song." He looked at Ethan, then Michael, as if he wanted them to help him. Michael opened his mouth to speak, but Pop said quickly, "Leave me alone. I don't feel good at all. I want to take a nap."

"Okay, James." Aunt Minnie waved Michael and Ethan away. "You boys take it into the hallway," she said, then whispered to Michael, "Did you call Dr. Janssen?"

Michael nodded and headed for the hallway. Ethan followed and asked, "How long has he been like that?"

"Like what?"

"Like *that!*"

"For a few months," Michael said. "But you couldn't know because you haven't been here."

"*Stop it*, Dad," Ethan snapped.

"Michael, what do you want?" the voice of Father Cliff came back to him. It was a question the priest had asked him a few months ago. "What do you *really* want now?"

"I want my old life back," Michael told him then. And it was true. He wanted his life to be what it was, with everything on course just as he'd expected.

Father Cliff looked at him with an expression of sadness, an expression that haunted him for days. "Honestly?" he asked. "You don't see anything good about your life now?"

Michael said, "No. What is there to see?"

"God at work," Father Cliff replied. "Stop and look around you. Stop and listen to your life."

Michael laughed then, thinking Father Cliff was giving him the old "stop and smell the roses" routine. He'd heard it so many times before from people who seemed to do nothing but smell the roses. But now, as Michael walked down the hall with Ethan, he realized that Father Cliff might've been talking about something else. Something that Ethan had figured out. Maybe Michael's anger was because Ethan had the audacity to do what he'd never had the courage to do. He didn't know. And it scared him to be left in the dark.

"Look, Ethan," Michael said in a conciliatory voice as they came close to the kitchenette door. "All I want is what's best for you."

"No, Dad," Ethan countered. "You want what you *think* is best for me. Which may not be the best for me. Do you see the difference? You think I'm being foolish, but I've learned a lot from my life this past year."

"Like what? Give me specifics."

Ethan groaned. "What do you want—a slide presentation? A detailed list? My experience can't be compartmentalized and categorized. Just once, can't you consider a way of thinking other than your own?" He was thoroughly exasperated. "Why do you have to be so ... so stubborn!" he cried out.

"*I'm* stubborn!" Michael countered. "You knew what was going on with me, with my dad, and you still left us high and dry."

"You gave me an ultimatum," Ethan reminded him. "Your way or the highway. So I took the highway. Now you resent me for making my choice."

"Because it was the *wrong* choice," Michael said, his voice getting louder.

Ethan held up his hand as if he was about to make a point, but he was cut off by another voice—high and shrill and unrecognizable because of its depth of anger.

"Stop it! Stop it right now!" Colleen shouted at them from the doorway. "I'm sick and tired of this fighting. If you want to talk about your differences, then *talk*—but stop this childish bickering! It's tearing me up inside and I don't want to hear any more of it! Do you understand? *No more.*"

Ethan was dumbfounded. Madison stood behind her mom in the kitchenette, looking shocked. Michael stared at his wife in amazement. The face of his wife, one he'd known and loved for so many years, was twisted red and splotchy with rage, made all the worse by a flickering fluorescent light overhead. Only once had he ever seen her lose her temper. It was a week after her father had lost a long battle against heart and kidney failures. Colleen had spent hours and hours at the hospital with him up until his death. When they phoned for her to pick up a few of his things, she couldn't bring herself to do it. They phoned two or three times. Michael didn't understand what was happening. He puzzled over what seemed like a simple task. He asked Colleen why she wouldn't go get her father's things. She wouldn't answer. He pressed the question until she finally shouted, in a red-faced rage, "*I hate hospitals and never want to set foot in one again!*"

That was a dozen years ago. Now, in this moment of rage, Michael recognized how brave Colleen had been all these months, coming to the Faded Flower with a smile and encouraging words, and deeply hating being there the entire time.

"Colleen ...," Michael said softly. He took a step toward her. She turned away, with clenched fists, and went to the stove. Her body shook as if it, too, had been scared by her outburst. She stood, looking down at a pot of boiling water. Then she flexed her hands and picked up a large spoon. She began to stir whatever was in the pot.

Madison gave her father and brother a look of rebuke. Then she went back to whatever she'd been doing at the counter behind her mother.

Ethan said quietly, "I'm sorry, Mom. Maybe it was a mistake for me to come." He backed away down the hall.

"It's my fault," Michael said, a near whisper. But Ethan was already out of earshot. Michael was assailed by a tremendous sense of loss, as if he'd been given an important test and had failed it.

Colleen sighed. Then she signaled Madison to take over the stirring. She wiped her hands on her apron and turned to Michael. "When are you going to snap out of this?" she asked in her usual tone. "You're already losing your father. Do you want to lose your son, too?"

The question was like a cold slap in the face.

He was saved from answering by Aunt Minnie, who strode down the hall toward him. "Did you talk to Dr. Janssen?" she asked.

Michael had forgotten completely and now reached for the phone in his pocket. "I'm sorry. I'll do it right now."

"Is something wrong?" Colleen asked.

"Pop has a high fever and says he's having trouble swallowing."

CHAPTER 11

DR. JANSSEN was a frumpy-looking woman with unruly white hair, large sad eyes, and a tiny mouth on a narrow chin. She confirmed that Pop's temperature was 102. Cause unknown. "Give him ibuprofen and make sure he stays hydrated. Keep an eye on him overnight. If there's no improvement, call me in the morning."

Pop certainly looked feverish. His cheeks were flushed and his eyes were narrow and glassy. He was watching them, but he didn't seem to be seeing them.

The family moved into the hallway.

"What about the swallowing? Does he have a sore throat?" Michael asked.

Dr. Janssen shook her head. "I don't think it's a sore throat. Problems with swallowing are a consequence of the Alzheimer's."

"So, no birthday celebration," Colleen said.

"You can celebrate his birthday," Dr. Janssen said, "but you'll have to do it without him."

"What's the point?" Michael asked.

Colleen and Madison dashed off to notify everyone about the cancellation.

Aunt Minnie looked shaken. "If he can't swallow, he can't eat."

Dr. Janssen touched her arm. "We'll watch and see."

———————————————◆———————————————

Michael stood alone at the foot of his father's bed. He gazed at the frail body under the sheet. His father had always been a strong, healthy man. Doting over him because of a fever seemed like an overreaction. But Michael had to keep reminding himself that Pop's mind and his body were not what they once were. He'd never really recovered from the fall he'd taken a couple of months back. He became exceptionally clumsy as his basic motor skills slipped. He suffered from colds more often. Every cough made Michael watchful. Colds often became pneumonia. Pneumonia was a primary killer of Alzheimer's patients. That, and the loss of the ability to swallow.

The father Michael had known all his life was slipping away from him. The gray, fragile old man sleeping in front of him was someone else.

Pop slept with his hands folded over his chest. *He could be in a coffin*, Michael thought with a shudder.

A mental checklist appeared in Michael's mind. Pop's will had been done, *check*. Funeral arrangements, *check*. Burial arrangements, *check*. His father wasn't always cooperative, but Michael was determined to get it all done while his father could participate.

"What Scriptures and hymns do you want for your funeral Mass," Michael had asked.

"I don't know. Surprise me," Pop had replied.

Right now, Michael wanted to talk to his father. Not *this* father, but the one he used to know. He wanted Pop's perspective about his life. He longed to hear Pop give his advice about why he was behaving like such a fool. "I don't want to lose my son. I don't want to alienate my family," Michael whispered. "But there's a deep anger that keeps churning inside of me."

"Who are you angry with?" he imagined Pop asking, because it's the sort of thing he would have asked. "Are you angry with me for getting old and becoming so helpless? I didn't do it on purpose, you know. I was supposed to be the wise old grandfather, living to be a ripe age and then passing quietly in my sleep. I wasn't supposed to lose my memory and my bodily functions."

"That's right," Michael would have admitted. "And I was supposed to work at my job until retirement and vacation with Colleen. Ethan was supposed to go to college and begin a lucrative career and start his own family. Madison, too, would meet some guy who'd love her to bits and have lots of money. And then there'd be grandkids. I had it all worked out. It was a good plan, a solid plan. But it went wrong."

Michael lowered his head. The sourness of self-pity settled on him. He felt pathetic and hoped no one would come in right at that moment.

God ... Michael began to pray. He stopped. Something moved just out of the corner of his eye. He tried to focus, looking at the dark shadows of the room, made even darker by the closed curtains on the French doors and the single lamp on Pop's bedstand.

Pop cleared his throat. "Are you all right? You don't look so good," he said. He was sitting up in his bed. *When had he done that?*

Michael came around the bed to ease him back. "Don't get up." Then he was aware that something wasn't right. Pop looked younger somehow. His eyes were alive and he wore a mischievous smile. Michael was certain that the light was playing tricks on him. Or he was dreaming.

Pop folded his hands on his lap and asked, "What's on your mind, son?"

He looked so earnest that Michael decided to play along with whatever hallucination he was experiencing. "I feel like I'm losing everything I care about."

"We've all had better years, I think," Pop said with a genuine smile.

Michael had to blink because Pop's wrinkles and age spots were fading. He was getting younger.

"As for statements like 'I'm losing everything I care about' ... well, your mother and I raised you better than that."

"What do you mean?"

Pop shook his head and Michael could see that his hair was darker.

"Tell me," Michael pleaded. "Even if this is a dream, I want to know what you mean."

"What did your mother and I teach you?" Pop asked. "You have to believe that God loves you more than you love yourself. He knows what he's doing even when you don't. It's easy to have faith when things are going well. It's harder when they aren't. It's even harder when you think God is being unreasonable."

"Unreasonable?"

He gestured to himself. "Don't you think it's unreasonable for me to end my life like this? I sure think so."

Michael nodded. *Yes, it is unreasonable.*

"Hope is unreasonable," Pop said.

"What hope?"

Pop's eyes went to a crucifix hanging on the wall by the bed. Even in the dim light, it looked radiant. "That was such an unreasonable thing for God to do. No death with dignity there."

"Does death ever have any dignity?"

"What does it matter?" Pop said. "It's what happens *after* that counts anyway."

Michael stood there for awhile. He reached out to touch his father's arm. His hand hung in mid-air. Then he realized he was standing back at the foot of the bed, his father still old and gray, asleep in front of him.

I'm losing my mind, he thought. And then he thought of Spooky Sally and her visions and wondered if God was playing a trick on him.

———————————— ◆ ————————————

Michael went to the Sun Room to help dismantle the surprise birthday setup. Colleen and Madison were in the kitchenette, wrapping up the various goodies for the freezer. He lingered, feigning a desire to help, but mostly wanting to be near both of the two women he loved the most. They were in their "get it done" mode and made it clear they didn't need him around. He knew the real reason.

He wanted to say something to them, to apologize for what had happened with Ethan. He opened his mouth to speak, but the words didn't come. He left them and went into the Sun Room to put some of the folding chairs away.

Michael was surprised to find Deacon Chuck already doing the work. "I wasn't sure where to put them, so I leaned them against the wall."

"That's kind of you. I'll take care of them."

Deacon Chuck had bushy white hair, a round face, and a kind expression. "How's your father?"

"Not well."

"Have some of this," Deacon Chuck said and went to a large bowl on a side table. It was filled with a red punch. Deacon Chuck smiled. "I brought this for tonight. I'd hate for it to go to waste. And I can't drink it alone."

Michael took the cup and drank. "Pretty good," Michael said.

"Let's sit," Deacon Chuck suggested. He went to two armchairs facing the large windows.

It wasn't lost on Michael that the chairs were favorites of Pop and his friend David, who was now recently deceased.

"It turned into a beautiful evening," the deacon said.

There was a patio beyond the glass with a fountain that had been turned into a giant planter. Lights now highlighted the leaves swirling around the fountain, scooted along by an autumn breeze. The sun had already slipped behind the mountains, leaving a blue shadow over everything.

"What can I do for you, Michael?" Deacon Chuck asked. "I think there's something. What do you want?"

Ah, that question again. *What do you want?* "I don't understand," Michael said.

Deacon Chuck didn't say anything for a moment. Then he took a sip from his cup and said, "I was once where you are. I had an iron grip on my life. I had strategized who I was and where I was going.

But, as they say, 'The best laid plans ...' I lost my business. I started drinking. My wife threatened to leave me. I had a heart attack. And every step of the way I thought I could fix whatever had gone wrong, like you might fix a hinge on a door or adjust a setting on a furnace. I was wrong. I hit rock bottom."

Michael was surprised by this information. In the time he'd known Deacon Chuck, he'd never heard about the man's past. Maybe he assumed Chuck was always a deacon.

"After I'd lost everything, I found everything." He laughed to himself. "Isn't that how it goes? Haven't we all heard the stories of people who had to lose everything to gain something more important? I think it must happen to everyone sooner or later. Only then can we see ourselves more clearly. For me, it came as a conspiracy."

Michael looked out at the fading sky. He felt skeptical about this conversation. It sounded too much like a pitch for a pyramid scheme or a testimonial for some point of view that may have worked for Chuck but had nothing to do with him. But politeness demanded that Michael ask a follow-up question. "What kind of a conspiracy?"

"Of grace," Deacon Chuck said. "Circumstances, coincidences, off-handed comments from friends, strange dreams, guilt, regret ... I began to see a connection to it all. It was a conspiracy."

Now Michael was on guard, wondering who Deacon Chuck had been talking to. Father Cliff? Or maybe any number of people Michael had complained to. *Have I really been that tiresome? How else can he know to say these things?*

"The whole thing was from God, of course," Chuck said. "Nobody else could have masterminded such a scheme. Nobody else would have cared to."

"And this conspiracy led you to some great life-changing revelation ... is that it?" Michael asked.

A quick nod.

Michael waited, but Deacon Chuck didn't say anything. "Well? Are you going to tell me what it was?"

Deacon Chuck drained his cup of punch. "I realized that we don't really belong here."

"Here?"

"In this world," he explained. "We're spiritual nomads, making our way to a final destination. That's why we're never really comfortable here. God won't let us get comfortable. He lets us hunger and yearn for something we can't find here, something that's just beyond our reach."

Michael shook his head. "I thought I had everything I yearned for," he said. "But God took it away."

Deacon Chuck turned to face him. His voice was plaintive as he asked, "You really thought you had everything you yearned for?"

Michael felt like a student under the stare of a stern teacher. He flinched. "Well ... yes."

"A stable job and a house and a good family ... was that it?"

"I never said my expectations were high," Michael said.

Deacon Chuck laughed. "The yearning I'm talking about is for something more permanent, more transcendent. Our jobs and possessions, even our families, can be like ... like painkillers to numb the real yearning."

"I'm not trying to be stupid," Michael said, feeling stupid. His thoughts leapt back to the weird hallucination of his father. Was he saying the same things as Deacon Chuck? Was this part of a conspiracy?

"It's an ache," Deacon Chuck continued. "An unsettled feeling as if you've forgotten something important or want something so terribly, though you're not sure what it is. It's a joy and sadness all wrapped up in one. God puts it inside of us. Sometimes it comes in isolated moments; sometimes it comes in a sudden rush of feeling." Deacon Chuck's voice grew softer. "Sometimes it hurts so much that we'll do whatever we can to make it stop. And other times we misunderstand what it is and try to quench it with the wrong things. That's what I did for years."

Michael fiddled with his punch cup for a moment and then asked, "But what does all this have to do with me?"

"I've been watching you ever since you came back to Hope Springs. You're like a fish caught on a hook—writhing and squirming, desperate to be free. You've had the hunger, the desire, and you seem to be trying to fulfill it the wrong way. You've gotten yourself hooked on the wrong line and you don't know what to do."

Michael went along with the analogy. "So, what's the answer for a poor, stupid fish?"

Deacon Chuck smiled. "If you don't know the answer, then I wonder what else God is going to have to do to help you."

"You make that sound like a threat."

"Let's not be sentimental about it, Michael," Deacon Chuck said. "God is a loving father—and loving fathers teach their children when they go astray. And it hurts sometimes."

Just then, a hand fell on his shoulder. "I'm sorry," Madison said. "Pop is awake. But he's really confused. Mom wants you to come to his room."

"Thanks." Michael stood up.

Deacon Chuck reached out and caught Michael's wrist. He looked as if he was about to say something, but didn't. He simply nodded.

Michael arrived at Pop's room in time to see Colleen and Aunt Minnie struggling to keep Pop in bed. He was fighting to get up.

Colleen said between grunts, "You have to stay in bed."

"The water. Do you hear it?" Pop asked, his voice filled with some inner alarm.

"Water?" Aunt Minnie asked.

"You have to kick the pipes to make it stop," he said.

Michael went around the bed and Aunt Minnie stepped aside. His father's pale face was a patchwork of red splotches. His eyes were dark and sunken. How was it possible that he could have aged so much in only a couple of hours? Michael put a firm hand on his shoulder. "We'll take care of the pipes, Dad."

Pop looked up at him, startled. "What? Who is that?"

"It's me. Michael."

"Michael who?"

The question felt like a slap. Pop had forgotten a lot of things over the past few months, but never him. He looked helplessly at Colleen. She shook her head.

"I'm your son."

"Oh," Pop said as if it was a point not worth arguing about. Then he looked at Madison, now standing at the foot of the bed. "Do I know who you are?"

"Yes, Pop," she replied. "I'm your granddaughter, Madison."

Pop frowned. "I don't think so."

"Of course I am." Madison was unfazed by his lapse of memory. "If I'm not, then who am I?"

Pop gazed at her. "The one who keeps stealing my watch."

Madison shook her head. "That's Father Cliff."

"Don't encourage him," Michael said to her. He turned to his father again, drawing close. "You really don't know who I am?"

Pop squinted at him like he'd been asked a trick question. "Why should I?"

Michael felt something lurch inside of him, like the feeling of butterflies he used to get when a roller coaster flew forward into its first drop. It was fear—a fear that his father might die tonight—he might die without remembering who Michael was.

Aunt Minnie touched Michael's arm. "He doesn't know. The harder you try, the more worried you'll make him."

Michael tried one last time. "You really don't recognize me?"

But Pop wouldn't look at him. He pulled the covers up close to his face and said, "I'm very tired. Can't you see I'm not feeling well? Leave me alone." He closed his eyes as if to make everyone go away.

Michael gazed at him a moment, then straightened up. "It's okay, Dad. Don't worry."

Colleen and Madison had quietly moved toward the door. Aunt Minnie joined them into the hall, followed by Michael.

"Does Dr. Janssen know about this?" Michael asked softly. "He's delirious."

"She knows. And she still wants to wait until morning," Colleen said.

Aunt Minnie added: "He was going to forget our names sooner or later. It's hard, but we have to look past it."

"*Hard* isn't the word for it," Michael said. "Will he come back from this? Does anyone know?"

Colleen looked tearful. "How can anyone know?"

"I asked him once if he remembered who I am," Aunt Minnie said. "'I know who you are,' he said. 'But I don't know who *I* am.'"

Michael was distressed. "You never told me that story."

"I didn't want you to get upset, like you are now," she said. "You've been here day after day. You must have seen this coming."

"I knew it was coming, but not now—not so fast," Michael said.

"It hasn't been fast," Aunt Minnie reminded him. She then looked as if she, too, saw no point in arguing.

"I'll stay with him tonight," Michael said. "You should all go home."

"All night?" Colleen asked.

Michael nodded.

"What about Ethan?" asked Madison.

"Where is he?" Michael asked.

"He came back for the party," Colleen explained. "When we told him it was cancelled, he said he might see us at home later." She faced Michael directly. "You two must call a truce."

Michael held up his hands as if yielding; it was as much of a concession as he could make. Ethan wasn't the priority. Right now, he wanted to talk to his father.

"I'll call Dennis so he knows what's going on," Colleen said. She gave him a quick hug.

Madison did the same. "I love you," she whispered.

Aunt Minnie looked worried. "Just sit with him," she said. "Pray with him." She spoke to Michael as if he hadn't been there all these months.

As she walked away, he suddenly felt like an actor who had walked onto an unfamiliar stage, playing a role he hadn't prepared for.

Michael went back into the room. He pulled Pop's wingback chair closer to the bed and sat down. The room was in shadows. The light from the bedstand seemed feebler than before, but spotlighted Pop's large-print Bible. It sat opened to the book of James, with a pair of reading glasses on top of the marked-up pages.

Gazing at his father, Michael thought of his dream, or the hallucination, from earlier. Pop had looked so much younger then. It was the father he knew as a boy. A montage of memories came to him then, dissolving one into another. There was Pop sitting on a webbed car seat, his armpits ringed with sweat, holding a dripping ice cream cone on a hot summer day. Pop making breakfast for the family on a Saturday morning. Pop carrying Michael on his shoulders during a long walk. Pop teaching him to play Wiffle Ball in the backyard. Pop putting calamine lotion on him after he'd sat in a patch of poison ivy.

"Turn on my program, will you?" Pop asked. He was looking at Michael with red-rimmed eyes.

My program was what Michael's mother had called her favorite soap opera. *Turn on my programs*, she'd say while wiping her hands on her apron. *Her stories*. Everything had to stop for them. "What program, Dad?"

"You know the one I like. On the radio."

Afraid his father might turn away from him again if he refused to comply, Michael reached over to the nightstand and pushed the button on the radio alarm clock. A baroque piece of classical music was playing on the local station. "How's that?" Michael asked.

He closed his eyes without answering.

"Dad," Michael began, his voice quivering from what he wanted to say. "I'm sorry for making you move out of your house. Maybe you were better off at home." What he was feeling was, *Maybe none of this would have happened if I'd left you alone.* Regret was a ball in his throat now. "I've botched everything with you, with Ethan, with everyone," he confessed.

This is ridiculous, he thought. A cliché. A deathbed scene with a penitent son. He'd seen it play out at the Faded Flower—kids who had neglected their parents, showing up at the last minute to receive parental absolution.

Pop slowly opened his eyes and looked at him. "It was only a house, you know."

"Only a house?"

"Not a home."

Michael frowned. "How can you say that? It was your home for years."

Pop's head moved, an almost imperceptible shake. "Not *home*. *Like* home." His voice became a whisper. "Shadows on the wall."

Michael was puzzled. "Do you understand what I'm saying? I'm trying to tell you that I'm sorry for a lot of things," he said, hoping the words would somehow penetrate the fog around his dad.

Pop cleared his throat. He spoke louder, his voice raw and raspy. "You need help."

"I guess I do," Michael admitted.

"You should talk to a priest or a doctor," Pop said. "Do you have any family in the area?" he asked in a worried tone.

"Dad, *you're* my family," Michael said.

Pop raised an eyebrow. "I think you're confused ..." He closed his eyes again. His breathing found a slow, sonorous rhythm.

A man speaking with the dulcet tones of a funeral director came on the radio to announce the next piece of music. Barber's *Adagio for Strings*. It seemed like an appropriate soundtrack for this pitiful moment in Michael's life.

Michael leaned forward, his hand finding his father's, his head on the cool sheets. They smell of Pop, he thought. He rubbed his burning eyes. Melancholic strings played through the tinny radio speaker.

I've missed the moment, he thought. *Isn't that how life is? You speak too soon, or you hesitate and speak too late—either way, the moment is gone, the opportunity lost.*

He thought of the moments. Life was filled with so many of them. Moments of longing, of yearning. Moments of innocence and of joy. They came without being beckoned. They left without being detained. They arrived and stood in front you; other times they were within sight, but just out of reach. Unpredictable and fickle and often out of place, like giggles at a funeral, or silence in a stadium full of shouting people. However they came and in whatever form they took, they had to be acknowledged and respected before they disappeared again. No amount of cajoling could prod or fix them. They could not be controlled.

Michael could no longer deny the truth. For all of his efforts to control his life, nothing changed the course of events that put him in that chair at that moment, sitting next to a father who didn't recognize him, at odds with his son, a stranger to his own life. The only control he had was the choices he made. The rest was in someone else's hands.

Deacon Chuck was right. Michael thought. *It's a conspiracy.*

He slumped back into the softness of the chair. It was Pop's favorite chair and he never understood why. The thing was ugly as sin. But, in this moment, he realized that it was so very, very comfortable. He closed his eyes just to rest for a minute.

"Michael."

He opened his eyes again. Had he fallen asleep? He must have. The red digits on the clock now said a few minutes past midnight. Wasn't it nine when he came in? He couldn't remember. Jazz was now playing on the radio. Pop's eyes were open, his expression serene.

"Did you just say my name, Dad?" Michael asked.

"Kick the pipes, will you?" Pop said. He sounded groggy. "They'll wake your mother."

"Okay, Dad. I will."

He reached over to pat Michael's hand. "You're a good boy. I could always count on you."

"Thanks, Dad."

Pop turned away again and slipped into a deep sleep.

Michael looked down at his father's hand, still resting on his own. *This is the moment I will remember. No matter what happens after this, I will hold onto this moment.*

And it became a prayer.

Chapter 12

It was one thirty and Michael had the feeling someone was watching him. He was still in Pop's chair and slowly opened his eyes. Pop was lying perfectly still. Michael leaned closer. Was he still breathing? He watched his father's chest. The blanket moved slightly, up and then down. He was relieved. He then remembered when Ethan and Madison were babies and he would slip out of bed on the pretense of going to the bathroom; instead, he would sneak in to make sure they were breathing. Only then could he go back to sleep.

He gently put his hand on Pop's forehead. It felt warm, but not as hot as it was before.

Out of the corner of his eye, he saw a shadow move. He quickly looked over. Ethan was sitting on the arm of the small sofa along the wall.

Michael put a finger to his lips and gestured for them to go out into the hall. Ethan nodded and followed him.

The hall was empty and dark, save for the light from the decorative electric candles that hung every few feet on the walls.

"Have you been here long?" Michael asked, still whispering.

Ethan shook his head. His cheeks were rose-colored and his hair was flecked with snow.

Michael dusted at the snow on Ethan's shoulders. He wore an old leather jacket that once belonged to Pop. "Have you been to the house?" Michael asked.

"I wanted to see how Pop was doing first," Ethan said. "He's not going to die, is he?"

"Dr. Janssen doubts it'll happen tonight." Michael looked into Pop's room. He could see his father on the bed. "But he may be taking a turn. Kind of a 'last lap.'"

There was an awkward silence. Michael knew what he had to say. He looked at Pop again, hoping to find some courage, and wondering why apologies were so hard to make. Finally, he said, "Ethan, this has been a hard time for us—for me."

"I know. But listen, Dad—"

Michael held up his hand to stop him. "No, please. Let me finish." He swallowed hard. "I'm sorry about everything that's happened. Between us, I mean." His voice sounded ragged to his own ears. "I'm sorry," he said again.

"No, Dad, *I'm* sorry," Ethan said. "I've been acting like a baby."

Michael shook his head in protest. "It's been me, Ethan. You were right about—"

"Really, Dad—"

"Will you listen for a minute?"

"No, I—"

And then they stopped and looked at one another and had to clamp their hands over their mouths to stifle the laughter.

"Are we going to argue over our apologies?" Ethan asked.

Michael's throat felt constricted, but he pressed on. "I want you to know that, no matter what you decide to do, you're my son and I love you and you're welcome in whatever house we're calling home."

He stopped and wondered, *Was that enough? Does he understand how much I mean what I'm saying?*

Ethan gazed at him with a look Michael recognized. A look every father wants to see from his son.

"I want to come home," Ethan said.

Michael sighed. "Then do it."

"You see, Dad—I have an idea."

This wasn't the direction Michael thought the conversation would go. "An idea?"

"You and I should start a business."

Michael did a double take. "What?"

"You handle the business side and I'll handle the hands-on work."

"What kind of work are we talking about?" Michael asked.

"A fix-it shop," Ethan said, his whole body becoming animated. "Phones, computers, anything technological. It's what I've been doing while I was gone. Hope Springs doesn't have one—well, not a good one."

"I don't know much about that. Not technical things."

"Neither did I. But my boss in New Mexico keeps telling me that I have a knack. He says I should open my own shop." Ethan smiled. "And you know business—how to set it up, get the word out. It's something to do until you come up with a better job."

"Well—" he didn't how to react. The idea was so unexpected. But ... why not? It could work.

"What do you think?" Ethan asked. He looked apprehensive.

"I think we should talk at home ... and figure it out." It was the sensible thing to say. But, in his heart, he felt a surge of excitement—a potential—that he hadn't felt in years.

A woman Michael didn't know came down the hall toward them. He then recognized her navy blue scrubs. She was a staff nurse.

"I'm going to check on James," she said. "You two are way past visiting hours."

"I'm a part-timer here," Michael said.

"Are you working now?" she asked.

"No."

"Then you should go home," she said. She continued on into Pop's room.

"Definitely a night-shift personality," Ethan said.

Michael signaled for Ethan to wait a minute. He followed the nurse into the room to watch her check Pop's vitals. She glanced at him, then got on with it. Pop hardly stirred.

"Ninety-nine point four," she reported in a whisper. "Blood pressure is 118 over 84. Seriously, you can go home. Dr. Janssen has told me to keep a special eye on him. We're going to bring in monitoring equipment. So, there's no point in all of us crowding him tonight, is there?" She arched an eyebrow.

"You know how to contact us," Michael said.

She nodded.

Michael was reluctant but thought of Ethan and decided they should go home.

They walked to Michael's little workroom where he kept his things. He put on his coat and dug around for his car keys, his hand brushing against some paper in his pocket. It was the letter from Cohen & Marx.

"What's that?" Ethan asked.

"An invitation."

Ethan looked at him quizzically.

He shoved the letter back into his pocket. "I think I got a better offer."

They stepped out into the cold night, father and son. They buried their hands into their coats and hunched their shoulders against the fat flakes of snow that drifted down and spun around like white moths.

"It should be Christmas," Ethan said happily.

"Yes," Michael said. "It feels like Christmas."

Perfectly Still

P OP LAY perfectly still while a nurse moved slowly around him. Her cold hands touched his forehead and then held his wrist. He tried to hold his breath, thinking that she would leave him alone if he did.

Music was playing somewhere nearby. Christmas music. Was it Christmas already? Time had become such a blur. Aunt Minnie took him for walks. He could still smell the smoke of a wood fire burning and enjoy the leafless trees with branches outlined by a coating of snow. The sun was a mere smudge through the clouds. *Snow.* All over his chest and legs. White like a blanket, and nearly as warm, too.

Colleen must have been nearby. Pop could smell her perfume. And Madison was there, too; she had the scent of something sweet, but he couldn't think of what it was. Minnie was saying something. He saw their faces close to his. Their smiles were so reassuring that he wanted to smile back. But the effort was exhausting. These days it took a lot of concentration to keep up with everything.

Sometimes he heard Michael's voice, sometimes Ethan's, and he wanted to ask them questions but couldn't.

All the same, he was glad to have them around. Wasn't it nice that Michael had quit his job so they could be closer? Families should be together, especially on a cold night like this. Not far away in some foreign land like his other son always was.

The nurse won. He simply couldn't hold his breath any longer—and he let go. It was such a long and luxurious breathing out. Almost like sinking into a hot bath in a big tub. His old house had one of those. He remembered how Linda insisted that he soak in it for a very long time after work. She brought him a cup of coffee and leaned on the porcelain to listen to him talk about his day, and then she would tell him everything the boys had gotten into.

It was so warm under his blanket of snow. He could feel the weight of it on his chest as he exhaled. It pressed down, helping him to let the breath go. He didn't think he had so much breath in his body to release. But there it went, swirling away from him in little eddies.

He felt a hand in his, but kept his eyes closed. Was it that nurse? No, it was probably the hand of Michael, with his long, slender fingers—just like his mother's. He should have learned to play piano with such long fingers. The hand squeezed his and his mind was filled with memories of the touch: holding hands with Linda, helping her out of the car, pulling her up from her garden work, taking the little hands of his boys in his as they crossed the street, holding their hands as he showed them how to swing a bat, firm handshakes when they left to start their lives. A million moments of the slightest touches all came back to him now.

A voice was speaking a language he had heard but didn't understand. *Si ambulávero in valle umbræ mortis, non timébo mala, quóniam tu mecum es.*[1] Someone was rubbing his forehead, a touch up and down, back and forth. Father Cliff. Who else could it be? *Redemptórem tuum fácie ad fáciem videas, et contemplatiónis Dei potiáris in sæcula sæculórum.*[2]

Then he felt another hand—rough—tugging at him gently, pulling him like Linda had so often done at the end of his hot bath in the long tub.

His breath was almost gone now. Why, it was such a feeling of purity, of cleansing, of clarity, that he wasn't sure he wanted to breathe in ever again.

THE END

---

[1] "Though I should walk in the midst of the shadow of death, I will fear no evils, for thou art with me" (English translation of Latin Vulgate, Psalm 22:4).

[2] "May you see the Redeemer face to face, and enjoy the vision of God for ever" (from the Prayer of Commendation).

The peace which surpasses all understanding.

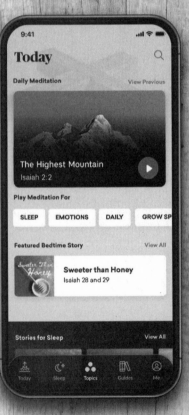

Now *easier to reach.*

Amen is the Catholic audio app that brings you beautif prayers, faithful meditation and nourishing Scripture to draw your mind, body and soul to rest in God...

and it's completely *free*

Learn more at AmenApp.org

Amen

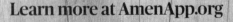